THE ANALYST

K.A. BRAGONJE

First published in 2018 by Alzena House

Visit the author's website at www.kabragonje.com

ISBN : 978-0-6483880-0-5

e-ISBN : 978-0-6483880-1-2

First Edition : August 2018

10 9 8 7 6 5 4 3 2 1

For Justin, Jake and Aaron

When everything seems to be going against you, remember that the airplane takes off against the wind, not with it.

Henry Ford

Chapter 1

Two nights ago, Emily Lee, a globe-trotting Financial Analyst, disembarked from a late night international flight and slipped back into Melbourne life unnoticed.

Her suitcases still piled up just inside the front door to her apartment. She'd felt like it'd been some time ago, but it had only been a couple of months since she was last here. In the prime of her career, she still loved the feeling of being handed a crisp new folder with the details of a new project contained inside.

The excitement still rushed through her, because new projects usually meant a new country and a new fully furnished apartment. To Emily, new assignments always felt like a new beginning, without the need for regular time off.

"Always working. You only need to worry about yourself," her sister Sophie said, her voice trailing off. "Freedom. I kind of remember what it felt like." Sophie jiggled her unsettled infant daughter on her hip.

Emily caught her sister looking around her dining room and shifted from one foot to the other. She hadn't had a chance to tidy up her mess before her sister arrived.

Stacked, empty noodle boxes sat to the side of the dining table. Left-over noodles clung to the outside of the boxes and onto the sprawled-out papers underneath. On the wall close by, all sorts of paperwork, printouts and photographs were pinned. Colored strings connected some of the items to each other.

Noticing her sister shrugging it off, Emily relaxed her shoulders.

"Freedom? If you call living out of a suitcase freedom." Emily tilted her head toward the stack of suitcases still unpacked near the front door.

While her sister's attention was distracted, Emily picked up the empty noodle boxes before any comments were made on her housekeeping... or lack of.

"Yeah, not that bit. But, you get to see the real world. Immerse yourself in the different cultures."

"I guess." Emily shrugged.

"I'm sorry for last night." Sophie wiped a tear from her cheek. "I just... had no one to turn to."

Her sister wasn't even meant to know she was back. He didn't even know she was in the country. But after her phone call last night, in tears, Emily had to console her sooner rather than later.

Emily wiped more tears from her sister's face. Grabbing her niece from her sister's hip, she pulled funny faces at her, but her niece wasn't too sure of her aunty, and her bottom lip quivered.

"It's okay. Do you want a cuppa?" Emily walked towards the kitchen. "Tea? There's got to be something here."

Emily rummaged through the pantry.

"A stiff drink would be great. But a tea would also be nice. Only if it's not too much bother."

Emily chuckled. "I'm sure we can manage that stiff drink. But I'm not too sure little bubba here," she tickled her niece's tummy, "would appreciate it."

The child cracked a little smile for a moment, then returned to her uncertain look.

"Ah, here we go. How does," Emily picked up a box and turned it over, "peppermint tea sound?"

"That'll be great, thanks."

"So, what's been going on?" Emily asked as she flicked the kettle on.

"Exhaustion is an understatement. Between Scarlett keeping me busy and worrying about Tom."

Emily froze, a teabag dangling above a cup. Her heartbeat sped up.

"Worried? How?" she asked, trying to sound calm, hoping her sister hadn't picked up on the nervous twitch in her voice.

Sophie waved her hand. "Oh, it's probably nothing."

Emily placed the teabag in the cup and faced her sister. "It's not nothing, though, is it?"

"I just worry when Tom leaves for his urgent overnight business trips. Sophie is so little, I worry if something goes wrong—"

"He always returns home, right? Yeah?"

"Yes. But when he comes home from these trips he's very secretive, distant. He pulls away when I try to touch him."

"He's probably tired. I know I'm tired for the first few days after a trip."

"No. There's something else going on."

"What makes you say that? He loves you both dearly. I see it in his eyes when you two are together. He dotes on you two."

"On his last trip the washing machine broke down mid cycle, water was gushing everywhere. I couldn't get hold of him on his cell phone so I tried his work." She wiped a tear and took a deep breath. "They belittled me and told me there's been no business trips, not that they'd send an office clerk on anyway."

Emily almost spilled hot water on the bench. She glanced at Sophie but her sister was busy wiping away another wave of tears.

"I thought he was—"

"That's what he's been telling me all along, too. I'd like to know what he actually does."

"Sounds like you need a break, get away for a little bit." Emily handed a cup of tea over.

"Thanks." Sophie took a sip and paused, the cup not far from her lips. "Do you think he's going to leave me and Scarlett?"

Emily looked into her sister's eyes. Pain and tears gazed back at her. She took a deep breath. "How can anyone leave two gorgeous women like you?"

Sophie waved Emily's comment off.

"I'm being serious. If he leaves you for another woman, I'll personally deal with him. He'd have rocks in his head if he left you. You're the best thing that's happened to him."

"I don't know. I don't know what to believe anymore."

"Look at your beautiful daughter. You can't tell me she hasn't got her mother's looks."

The corner of Sophie's lips turned up a little. Her daughter reached for Sophie but Sophie turned her attention to Emily's table, and Scarlett began to whimper.

"So, what are you working on here?" Sophie asked as she picked up a piece of paper.

"A little something on the sideline."

"A little something?" Sophie chuckled. "It looks more serious than that. You on another case?"

"Kind of. I don't want to bore you with my stuff."

"Hey, it'll be a welcome relief." Sophie grabbed her daughter, giving in to her fussing.

"I warned you." Emily smiled. "A job came through the email system. The sender looked familiar but it wasn't one of our normal clients. Anyhow, the boss brushed it off. Reckoned he had more important projects for us to work on than some poor farmer who'd allegedly had his land taken by the bank."

"That's terrible. I think I remember something about that. It was in the paper the other day. Was it a farmer from the North-East area of the state?"

"That's the one. I didn't feel comfortable with it being pushed to the side. So, in my own time, I've been conducting my own research."

"Busy is an understatement. You looking after yourself?"

"Yes, Mom." Emily winked at her sister.

"Looks like it with those noodle boxes you hid."

"It's quick, filling, and has veggies in it."

Unable to come up with a comeback, Sophie shook her head and smiled.

"It looks like you've made some progress." Sophie squinted at the wall of connected notes.

"I think so. And I don't like what I've found."

"Okay." Sophie raised her eyebrow, gesturing for Emily to continue.

"I've got to go over everything one last time before I hand it in to my boss. But it goes right to the top. I want to be certain first."

The high-pitch annoying news music played at a higher pitch than what Emily had set the television to. She slightly turned her head to see what was so important. *Another report of a shooting happening over in America,* she wondered.

A female local news reporter in a newsroom appeared, her tone somber as she commenced her segment. "Breaking news just in. There's a hostage situation occurring right now at the Bank of Victoria headquarters in Collins Street, Melbourne."

Emily's eyes glued to the television.

"Will this-"

"Shh." Not taking her eyes off the television screen, Emily held her hand up to her sister.

The news reporter continued, "Information is sketchy. But we believe at least one employee has been taken hostage."

The news reporter pressed her finger against her ear. She nodded periodically. Her attention returned to the camera, and she stretched her hand to receive a sheet of paper that was being handed to her.

"Sorry, everyone," the reporter continued. "Further information just in. A farmer, Harry Fry, from North-East Victoria, has claimed responsibility for today's situation at the Bank of Victoria headquarters in Melbourne. I'll now read you the statement issued by the hostage-taker. These are the words of the hostage-taker, and not those of this broadcasting channel."

The reporter scrutinized the piece of paper before reading out loud, "Today we unite as one. For too long now, the corrupted banks have done what they want, when they want, without a care in the world for our country's law and policies. What's even worse, the government are turning a blind eye to the corruption that's happening on their doorstep. No one in power is asking the banks the tough questions, no one is keeping them accountable.

"They're stealing the properties of hardworking

Australians, the majority of whom have never defaulted in their life. My family's farm, which has been in our family for many generations and was run very successfully, was also stolen from us in recent weeks.

"The banks are not providing any of us with any evidence to support their actions.

"Some of my farming friends who have had their land stolen from beneath their feet are no longer with us. Their pride and the fight against the big banks proved to be too much for them to take on.

"Today I'm taking a stand for these property owners, and their families, who cannot speak up. It's time for the government to wake up and take notice of what the banks are doing to our country and get some balls and do something about it."

The reporter faced the camera. "The words of a very unhappy farmer." She shuffled some papers in front of her before continuing. "Police have informed us the two blocks surrounding the Bank of Victoria have been closed off to all traffic. Everyone is advised to restrict all unnecessary travel to the banking district until the situation is resolved. We will bring you more news as it comes in."

Advertisements returned to the television. Emily took a couple of steps toward the screen. Her eyes drifted across to her collaged wall behind the dining table, a wall she'd covered in photographs, notes and printouts. She focused on a central photograph of a middle-aged man.

"I... I don't believe it," Emily whispered.

Chapter 2

He positioned his sniper on the window ledge.

Lucky thirteen, he thought.

Thirteen hits since he'd been discharged from the Army two years prior. Before that, in his previous life, you couldn't count his kills on your fingers and toes. You'd need three or four sets of digits, at least, to get close to his total hits. He had been a top marksman in his crew until he was court-martialed and discharged.

"Tom, do you have the target in sight?" a voice with a Chinese accent asked on the other end of his headpiece.

He zoned in on the target's window and made some final adjustments to his sniper. A light came on inside the apartment. Perfect.

Tom noticed movement in front of the window as the curtain was pulled back. The target stepped in front of the window.

He gasped.

"You sure this is the target?" Tom asked into his microphone.

"Do you have a clear shot?" the voice in the headpiece demanded.

The target faced the window, her face visible. A small infant, no older than twelve months, cried in her arms. It seemed she was trying to calm the infant down, pointing to something outside the window, directly at his location.

Tom tried to shrink farther beneath the window ledge, although he was already well hidden from his viewpoint.

"I repeat, do you have a clear shot?" The command was deafening in his ear.

Tom returned to his position and stared at her through his scope. He'd never known where she lived or what she did for a job. Tom had tried countless times to get her to let them go to her place. She was rarely home, and when she was she always insisted they meet secretly at some swanky upper-class city motel.

A smile appeared on his face as he remembered how he loved the way her hair flowed over her shoulders and down the front of her chest. How she would giggle when he would brush her hair away from the side of her face to steal a kiss before she would abruptly leave the motel room, leaving him alone in there to reminisce on the previous night's rendezvous.

He shook his head and snapped back to the job at hand.

"There's a problem," Tom said.

"You need to take the shot. NOW! Do I need to remind you there'll be consequences if you don't take the target out?"

"The target has an infant in her arms. I don't take out kids!"

"I don't care! She's in our way! Take care of her. If you must, take them both out. NOW!"

Looking through his scope, he could see something had caught her eye inside her apartment. She turned her head away from him.

A noise in the distance caught his attention. He lifted his head and cocked his ear in the direction of the noise. Not too far away, sirens blared and tires screeched as the cars took the corners quickly. It sounded like they were turning from the west side of the city square heading towards the city center. Some were a little farther away, but they still sounded like they were heading his way.

"Shit! They were quick! I haven't even-"

He'd been familiar with sirens sounding soon after leaving jobs, but not before a job was taken out.

"No, it's just a coincidence," Tom said quietly.

"Take the shot. Get out of there now! You have ten seconds to clear the hell out of there," demanded the voice on the other end of the earpiece.

Tom pulled the trigger.

Chapter 3

A loud shatter came from behind Emily. She dropped to the floor and huddled in a corner. All was quiet except for the TV. Looking around, Emily found her sister on the floor, cradling her daughter. Both were quiet. Emily crawled over the shards of glass to her sister.

"Soph," she screamed, shaking her sister.

There was no response, not even a whimper from Scarlett. She got up on all fours and cradled her sister's head, rocking back and forth, tears streaming down her face.

"Nooo, Soph. Stay with me. You can't leave me, not now. I... I need you."

Emily pulled her niece back. Sophie's shirt was soaked in blood. Her daughter's blood. A single shot through her niece's head and through to her sister's chest. A pool of blood formed around Sophie's body. Emily tried to find a pulse. Nothing.

"Nooooo," she screamed.

Emily looked over at her sisters' body and whispered, "The son of a bitch who did this is gonna pay!"

She leapt up and picked up her telephone receiver. Dead. Dropping it, she raced to her cell phone. No service.

Strange, both were working earlier, she thought as she checked her cell phone reception again. Still no signal.

Unplugging her cell from the charger, she also grabbed her cell phone backup battery and slipped it into her pocket. She looked at her watch. It was mid-morning.

As fast as she could, Emily took photos of all the paperwork on her wall and dining room table. She flicked through the settings until she came across her backup application. A window box appeared. It read,

Cannot connect to the Internet

"Seriously? No phone and no internet. What is going on?"

Her television began to flicker. Frustrated, she thumped the side of it. It flickered a bit more. "Now you're going to flip out on me," she said and banged the television again. The television reception returned to normal signal strength.

Checking her cell phone again, she noticed her reception was still down.

"The landlord is going to kill me," she said, standing in the middle of her living room and taking one last look at her apartment.

Her eyes fell to her sister and niece. A single tear rolled

down her face. Composing herself, she wiped her eyes, smearing her sister's blood all over her face. On her way out, she grabbed her jacket and bag, checking to ensure her backup charger was in it.

Running down the narrow, minimally lit corridor, she banged on her next-door neighbor's door. Emily kept glancing over her shoulder as the deadbolts were being unlocked. A frail Asian woman opened her door.

"Call the police," Emily said.

The woman looked Emily up and down and proceeded to close the door. Emily stopped her. The woman took a step back.

"Please. My sister and niece have been shot. Someone has fired shots into my apartment."

The woman's eyes rolled sideways before she stared at her feet and shook her head. "No, sorry. I can't."

A single shot was fired and the woman crumpled to the ground.

"Frick!" Emily took a few steps away staring at her neighbor.

The woman's body began to slide back, away from the door. Emily broke into a sprint down the hallway towards the elevators. She fumbled with her phone as she dialed the Police.

"This call cannot be connected," an automated response advised on the other end.

"Damn it." Emily slid her phone into her jeans pocket.

A second shot rang out. Emily ducked and felt the bullet

whiz past her ear. She turned around. A muscly, shaven headed man stood outside her neighbor's apartment. His gun pointed at her. The elevator door chimed and the doors opened. Before it was fully open, she threw herself inside the elevator, watching out for its occupant.

"Quick. Shut the doors," she yelled, keeping her eyes on the shooter. A scar stretched down the left side of his face.

The young man she'd narrowly avoided barging into had a backpack hanging over one shoulder and books in the nook of his arm. He stood unmoving near the elevator's control pad, looking at her before glancing out into the hallway at the armed man, now half way down.

"Quick," Emily screamed.

At long last he repeatedly pressed the close-door button. The shooter raised his gun at her.

Come on, come on, she thought.

It felt like the doors were taking forever to close. The shooter aimed and quickened his pace.

Emily clambered to a side wall and pressed her body up against it, trying to make herself paper-thin. She peered out into the hallway. A bullet bounced off the door. Emily flinched back. The doors closed.

"Going down?" the young man asked.

"I'm not going up."

"Bit of an eventful morning?" he asked, looking her up and down once again, drawn to her blood-soaked clothes.

"You mind your own business and I'll mind mine."

"No worries, love. Just making conversation. After all, I did just save your life."

"Thank you," Emily managed to get out to be polite. She cast around her mind for a bit of normality. "What're you studying?"

The man looked down at the books cradled in his arm. He blushed. "Ah, just a masters in Cyber Security with an interest in Business Intelligence in the financial sector."

"A masters? Get out of here. You look too young to be completing your masters."

His face turned a deeper shade of crimson.

Emily looked up at the digital display. Level three.

"You enjoying the course?"

"It's interesting." He looked up towards the digital display as well before continuing. "Did you hear about the hostage situation?"

"Hostage situation?" She shrugged her shoulders.

"At the bank headquarters."

Emily shook her head.

"It's not surprising. It was bound to happen sooner or later."

"How so?" she asked.

"That bank has been corrupt for a long time. It was only a matter of time."

"Only a matter of time for what?"

"Yeah." He looked down at her. "The current director is corrupt. He's obviously ticked off the wrong person today."

"Why do you say that?"

The elevator chimed. "Ground floor," a recorded voice said

over the speaker system. The doors opened.

"You know more than you're letting on." He winked at her and stepped into the lobby.

Emily grabbed his arm. "I've been investigating this man for the last few weeks. Exactly, how corrupt are we talking?"

"Hey, lady, I'd love to chat to you. But I have to get to Uni." He pulled his arm from her grip and jogged through the lobby and out the doors.

Emily looked around. No one unusual here. No one standing around trying not to look too conspicuous. Just busy people going about their everyday life. She pulled her jacket on and cinched it tight around her.

Stepping outside, she was dazed for a moment, blinded by the sun's glare. It didn't take long before she adjusted. The first thing she noticed was that people were running past her, pushing her on their way past, many of them screaming. She turned around. The gunman was standing in the middle of the lobby. His arm extended as he swung the gun around the foyer.

Emily looked around. At a nearby tram stop she spotted the university student standing at the edge of a growing crowd. His head was bobbing to music. Everyone at the tram stop seemed oblivious to the commotion behind them.

She looked back into the lobby. He was closer. The gun was now poised at her. She ran across the street, abruptly stopping traffic, not caring about the cars beeping their horns at her.

"There's a gunman. Get out of here," she screamed, waving

her arms.

Some people ignored her.

An older suited man glanced behind Emily and saw the gunman standing outside the apartment building, gun poised in their direction.

"We need to get everyone out of here," she told him.

"Everyone. There's a gun."

A few turned around and saw the gunman over Emily's shoulder. Some of them screamed "gun" before running away. Chaos erupted around Emily. People were running every which way.

The gunman no longer had a clean shot at her.

Still, a shot rang out. A young suited woman crumpled to the ground.

Emily looked down the tram line. No tram. She turned on the spot. Lost. Disorientated. Tall buildings on large city blocks surrounded her.

Chapter 4

Fu crouched behind his newest recruit.

"Show me what you've got," he whispered.

The recruit cracked his neck before lining his target up and waited. A scar on the side of his face indicated he wasn't a stranger to these situations.

Although they were within easy shot of Tom, Fu didn't want them to be seen. Not when both recruits were armed.

No, this had to be quick and clean. There was no room for error. After all, too much was riding on this.

"Come on," Fu whispered.

His recruit turned and glared at Fu. Fu gestured an apology with his hand and sat back a little, but still close enough to be able to see everything. He looked on as his recruit returned his concentration to Tom, lining him up.

Fu didn't like this position. He couldn't see Tom's target. But this was the first and would likely be the last opportunity to get her. After today, it was going to be a lot harder. They'd have to study her new routines, and too many people would have found out by now that she was back in the country. She would scarcely be alone anymore.

Fu watched as Tom made the shot, placed his rifle in a bag and stood up. The recruit fired and hit his target. Tom fell over the balcony and disappeared.

"Unlucky thirteen." Fu patted the recruit on his back. "Don't get caught. I'll be in touch."

The recruit packed away his firearm. Still crouching, Fu headed for the door.

Careful not to touch anything with his hands, he left the room. He casually walked down the corridor to the last door and disappeared into another room.

Walking into his boardroom, his arms extended, he announced, "Two down."

Before him sat thirteen suited people from diverse cultures. Fu received confused looks from some, while others nodded and exchanged smiles with the persons seated on either side of them.

Around Fu, the room was adorned with various oriental artefacts and paintings, many brought in from all over Asia from acquisitions of one kind or another. Each piece held some form of significance to him. Red drapes lined one side of the room, in sharp contrast with the pitch-black walls.

Fu took his place at the top of the table.

"What about the others?" a Middle Eastern man seated to Fu's right asked.

"Abdul, they're being dealt with." Fu took a sip from a glass of water.

"We need this investment to go through." Abdul thumped his fists on the table. His eyes fixed on Fu, he added, "We cannot afford for anything to stop it."

"I understand. There's a lot riding on this transfer. Everyone has something invested in this... arrangement. Andrew," Fu turned to his left. "Will the transfer be completed on time?"

Andrew tugged at his tie and cleared his throat before answering. "All paperwork was submitted two days ago. I've been ensured this transfer is a high priority. All going well, it should be transferred through to your Corporation by the end of the week." Andrew shifted in his seat, avoiding eye contact with everyone.

"What aren't you telling us?"

"Your niece-"

"Adoptive niece," Fu corrected him.

"Okay." Andrew collected his thoughts before continuing. "Emily. She's been rather intrusive with her nosey questions. It's been causing some unnecessary attention. Some of my staff are catching wind and starting to ask questions."

"You've got a niece poking around?" a man with a heavy Eastern European accent asked.

Fu lent on his arm, his finger tapping the side of his face, and pondered for a moment.

He turned to Andrew. "Your staff. They're for you to keep

quiet. As for Emily, she shouldn't be causing any more problems. Your headquarters. There's a... situation."

"Situation?"

"Have you not seen the news?"

"No, I've been in meetings all day."

"Go on, pull up the news headlines." Fu gestured for him to look it up.

Andrew opened his news application on his cell phone. His face dropped.

"Sharon," he whispered.

"That's right. I wonder how your wife is going to like the headlines tomorrow."

Andrew looked at Fu with a confused expression.

Fu ignored him and addressed everyone else in the room. "Everyone has benefited quite substantially from these acquisitions. I trust you're satisfied with your new land parcels. The last parcel shall... what do the westerners say? Be the icing on the cake."

Everyone chuckled, except for Andrew, who avoided all eye contact and stood up. While still chuckling with everyone, Fu pushed Andrew back into his chair.

"Now, gentlemen, and lady." He nodded in the direction of the only woman seated at the opposite end. "If there are no questions, please adjourn to the room next door for some refreshments."

Fu remained standing at the head of the table, exchanging nods and pleasantries with the group as they walked past.

"I hope you've been satisfied with the service Bank of Victoria has been able to provide you." Andrew extended an open hand to Fu.

He towered over Fu, whose turn it was to shift uncomfortably on his feet.

Fu looked at his hand and then looked up. "You've achieved what was asked of you. For that, we are grateful."

Andrew looked at his hand then back to Fu, and with a nervous twitch lowered it.

"If we can be of any more service..." He lowered his head.

"That'll be all. Take this," Fu reached for an urn sitting behind him. "As a goodwill gesture, for your service to the Corporation."

The urn was about thirty centimeters high and had been given to him by a family who'd had it passed down to them through the generations.

"No, no, I can't." Andrew stepped away.

"I insist." Fu pushed it into Andrew's hand. "There are many more where this came from. See yourself out. Be safe out there. It's not the same world we grew up in."

Andrew looked at him with a baffled expression. Fu winked and gave him a crooked smile before closing the door behind him.

Chapter 5

In the chaos, Emily heard a male's voice yell out, "Quick, this way."

She was frozen, her eyes glued on the shooter. Next thing, she felt her arm being pulled, and her legs moved, stumbling to keep her upright.

"We meet again," she said when she clocked his face.

"Funny that," he said, letting her go so he could re-adjust the books under his arm. "Now, less chatter, more running."

A bullet hit a metal street sign near Emily's head. She ducked as she ran along the street. The gunman was still in her line of sight.

"Come on! We're sitting ducks here," the youngster yelled, now a few steps ahead of her.

Another shot fired; moments later, the shop window next to them shattered.

"What's up?" Emily asked, noticing her rescuer had stopped.

He ignored her, instead grabbing her arm as she caught up to him, his grip tighter. He began running again, his pace quicker than hers. She was struggling to keep up. Her breath sounded hoarse as she fought to get it under control.

In recent years, her training and fitness had taken a secondary spot to make way for her growing career. In the beginning, it only interfered a little, but it wasn't long before her career swallowed all her available time and Asian noodle boxes replaced kale and quinoa salads.

He dragged her into an alleyway, showing no signs of slowing down.

"Can we stop? Please," Emily asked a few steps in.

"Do you want to be killed today?"

Emily pulled her arm free and bent over, her hands on her hips, gasping for air.

In between deep breaths, she said, "I need just a minute."

"We don't have a minute."

She could still hear the gunman shooting at anyone and everyone. "There's got to be more than one gunman out there."

Carefully, Emily edged to the mouth of the alleyway and peered back into the street. Dead bodies were everywhere, some on the ground, some slumped over steering wheels or railings. It was carnage.

People screamed as they scattered out of the gunman's way. He had his sights on something. Emily pressed her back against the wall and followed his line of sight.

No. No, he's not, is he?

In the gunman's path, a mother was lying over her child, covering her child's eyes and ears with her own hands.

"No," the mother yelled as the gunman stopped in front of them.

He raised his gun and the mother stared into his gun barrel.

The gunman raised his other arm, a little lower than the one aimed at the mother. She huddled over her child a little more, shaking her head at him. Two shots rang out and he lowered both arms as the mother fell onto her child.

Stunned, Emily edged away from the street and deeper into the alleyway.

"I didn't think so. This way," her rescuer instructed, already on the move.

She looked over her shoulder, in the direction of the mother and child, before running after her rescuer.

Chapter 6

A couple of office doors up from Fu's boardroom, his newest recruit leant on the door frame as he drew on his cigarette, his ear cocked towards the boardroom while he pretended to unlock the door.

It won't be long and I'll be back in the comfort of isolation. Away from civilization, the local wildlife the only thing keeping me company, he thought as he drew on his cigarette.

He looked at his watch, then over his shoulder towards the boardroom door. Still alone in the corridor, but he wasn't sure for how much longer. He'd already been lingering out there for too long. It increased his risk of being caught, being recognized. He liked being a ghost, in and out, no one seeing him.

He inhaled the last bit of his cigarette before dropping the butt to the floor.

A door creaked as he snubbed the cigarette out with his shoe.

The recruit lowered his head and angled it until the boardroom door came into view. It wasn't long until he saw a man in a business suit trying to wrangle with the door while holding onto a folder and a large oriental urn.

The recruit faced his own door handle and pretended to be locking it when he heard the boardroom door latch echo down the hallway.

He counted to ten and turned around. His target in sight, he followed him, closing in on him with each step. Just as he came level, he fell into step with his target.

"Here, let me help you," the recruit offered as he reached for the urn. "You look like you could do with some help."

The businessman pulled his shoulder around, trying to block this stranger from grabbing the urn.

"We're both heading to the same place." The recruit pointed to the elevator. "Please, let me help."

The businessman stopped and looked him up and down, deciding whether to hand the urn to him. His gaze stopped at the stranger's gloved hand.

"Oh, these? They just hide my eczema. It's not contagious, I'm just conscious of how they appear in public."

The business man thought for a moment before replying, "Thank you, but only until we get to the elevator."

"Understood. Just trying to help a neighbor."

"Oh. No. I don't live here."

"My apologies. I'm Fred." The recruit extended a hand over a friendly smile. "I'm a new resident on this floor, still learning who's who around here."

The businessman, flustered, shook his hand. "Andrew. I must admit, you don't look like a Fred. New to the city?"

They resumed walking down the corridor.

The recruit ignored his comment. *Cannot get personal with anyone, let alone my targets,* he thought.

"This looks like a nice specimen." The recruit turned the urn around.

"Don't know what I'm going to do with it yet."

"A smart man like you will no doubt find somewhere for it."

Andrew chuckled.

They approached the elevator and waited for it to reach their level. It didn't take too long before the elevator chimed and the doors opened.

"After you," Andrew gestured.

"Uh, no." The recruit took a couple of steps back and waved his hand in front of him. "You first. I'm taking the stairs. I don't like those things. You know, claustrophobic and everything."

Andrew nodded, seeming to understand.

The recruit watched Andrew as he stepped inside the elevator. He placed his folder on the floor in between his legs and pressed a button on the wall. Andrew extended his arms, ready to grab his urn.

The recruit stepped forward.

The doors were closing.

He pulled out his gun. Andrew eyes widened when he saw it pointed at him.

Do not hesitate. This is why we don't learn names, the recruit thought to himself.

He shot Andrew square in the chest, twice, moments before the doors closed shut. A loud thump came from inside. He assumed it was Andrew falling to the ground.

Standing in the corridor alone, he stared at the closed door, his gun still poised. Listening. The elevator continued to descend. He waited a bit longer. The elevator doors didn't open.

Somewhat content, he slipped his gun back under his jacket and walked back up the corridor. He was sure someone would've opened their door after the incident. But all the doors remained shut. Not a soul cared.

Opening the door to Fu's boardroom, he looked around. He was alone. Behind the double doors at the other end, he could hear laughter and glasses clanging together.

"So, this is how the rich live?" he whispered.

To his right, along the far wall, a set of closed double doors sat alongside a buffet. In the center of the buffet there was a noticeable gap.

He almost had the urn back in place when an eruption of laughter exploded from the other side of the double doors. He jumped, almost dropping it.

His hands shook as he placed it on the buffet.

Two people on the other side of the door were talking, their voices muffled. He stood there, not moving, watching the door handles.

They moved on.

Letting his breath out, he left the room the same way he found it. Untouched, and not an ounce of evidence he was ever there. Just the way he liked it.

Chapter 7

Bluestone cobbles lined the narrow alleyway.

Emily looked ahead of them. A dead end.

"Umm, we have a problem," she said in between breaths.

"Do we?"

The youngster stopped opposite an old metal door. Nothing welcoming about it. Emily looked around. No signwriting. No gunman. Just the stench from overflowing trashcans that lined the dark and dank bricked walls.

He opened the door, pulled her inside and locked the door behind them.

Emily placed her hands on her hips as she tried to catch her breath.

"Come on," he instructed again.

He was already running down the long, barely lit corridor. Emily sighed, conjured what little energy she had left, and ran after him. Her legs screamed, her heart was racing. She pushed through, gritting her teeth.

When this is over, I need to re-commence my Muay Thai training, she thought as she ran after him.

She didn't know how far they'd run when she saw him stop underneath a little light that illuminated another door.

"I don't know what you're into," he said to her. "I don't want to know. What I do know is that you're not from around here. I'll get you as far away from that gunman as I can. It'll buy you some time. Then you're on your own. Whether you get through today is up to you. Okay?"

Emily tried to talk, but her breathing was still too heavy. She nodded.

He opened the door, and a brightly lit room greeted them.

Chapter 8

Fu slouched in his chair at the head of his boardroom table. His older brother Tao sat to his side.

The curtains were drawn, the only lighting coming from a handful of red lamps placed around the room.

Fu pressed a button under his table and two security guards entered through the main entrance, each man the width of the doorway. In between them, they dragged a scrawny man in his mid to late thirties. His shirt was barely hanging over his shoulders. Blood had soaked into the front and back of his shirt. His head was bowed, all the fight gone out of him.

Fu nodded at the men and they let go of the body, which fell in a heap on the floor.

The man moaned.

"Up," Fu demanded.

The man kept his head bowed and tried to get up but his body refused to cooperate with him.

A security guard kicked the man in the ribs. The injured man grabbed his side and yelped in pain.

"You got a hearin' problem? Up. That is, unless you want to take your last breath right there."

The injured man moaned as he arched his back and moved onto all fours.

"I don't have all day. On your feet. Now."

The man staggered onto his feet, the top half of his body swaying. He kept his head bent forward.

"Look at me," Fu said.

The man slowly raised his head until he was looking into Fu's eyes.

"Do not ever cross me again. Next time you won't be given another chance. Clear?"

The man nodded and looked down at his feet.

Fu stared at him with disgust.

He swept his hand towards the door as he said, "Get him out of here."

A guard placed a black cloth bag over the man's head before escorting him from the room.

Fu took a deep breath in and breathed out slowly before turning his brother. Tao's eyes were wide open.

"Well, Tao." Fu smiled.

His brother returned the strained smile.

"I, I don't believe..."

"The things I've got to do to keep everyone in line? How are we going this month?" Fu asked as he unbuttoned his jacket.

Tao opened his laptop.

"Very good. Even better when we stop being screwed by little punks who think they can outsmart us."

"Yes. Well. They'll never learn." Fu leant back in his chair.

Tao punched some keys on the laptop and spun it around for Fu to see. A few graphs were displayed on the screen.

"What am I lookin' at here?"

Tao pointed to the first graph. "This one here–"

"I don't care what they say." Fu pushed the laptop back. "How are we going?"

Tao sighed and turned the laptop back around to face him.

"We're doing really well. We're on par with our forecasts."

"On par?"

"Yes."

"We're not exceeding?"

"No. Not quite."

"Any new territories we've taken control over?"

Tao closed the laptop and looked at Fu.

"No. The sales from our dealers are down a little."

"What about the stock going to them?"

Tao paused. Opening up the laptop, he pretended to be looking up the figures. "The stock requests are up, along with the quantities."

"They're up! The little shits." Fu thumped his fists on the table. "When will they fricken' learn? Do they think we're stupid or somethin'?"

Tao didn't reply.

"Right, I need to sort them out. Pull them back into line. Again. This time they'll learn to stop shortchanging us."

Fu sat quietly for a while, thinking before he continued. "Some changes need to happen around here."

"What are you thinking?" Tao asked.

The door opened.

Fu looked up to see the two guards re-enter the room, both wearing clean shirts. They walked around the table until they were standing behind Tao.

Looking up at them and back to Fu, Tao asked, "What's going on?"

"Changes." Fu stood up.

"I... I don't understand."

Fu continued to walk towards the door. Without turning around, he clicked his fingers and said, "Bring him.

Chapter 9

It took Emily's eyes a moment to adjust to the brightness. The white light slowly gave way to a department store room. Racks of women's clothes surrounded her.

"What are we doing in a department store?" Emily asked.

"Here. I think these will fit you." Her rescuer thrust a handful of clothes into her arms. "Put these on. Your old clothes in this bag." He handed her a backpack. "Bring this bag back here."

"I can't just walk out of here without paying for these."

She glanced at one tag. A plain t-shirt with a hefty price tag. "I can't afford these."

"You're wasting valuable time. Do you want to draw attention to yourself with all that blood over you?"

Okay, he had a good point there.

"Where are the changing rooms?"

He pointed to the left of the building. Emily followed his gaze. She saw the fitting room sign dangling a few aisles over.

"Grab the one closest to the entrance. Be quick."

Still in a daze, she navigated the aisles. Looking over her shoulder, she saw her rescuer bob down. She didn't feel right about any of this. A stranger. Forcing her to shop lift. A gun man attempting to take her life.

Emily looked around the changing room. It was unmanned. She breathed out a sigh of relief and found the closest cubicle, a room set aside for the elderly and disabled. She snipped the door locked and placed the clothes on a chair. Mirrors on three sides of the tiny cubicle greeted her blood-soaked clothes.

Tears rolled down her face as she pulled her blood-soaked shirt off and held it up to her face. She closed her eyes and saw her sister and niece lying there. Alone.

A distant knock made her open her eyes again. She was back in the changing room, clutching her blood-soaked shirt. Emily heard the knock again. Louder, this time. On her door. She snipped it open, slowly.

"You ready yet?" The youngster's curly red locks appeared through the doorway.

"Give a woman a minute."

"You've got thirty seconds." He closed the door.

Emily struggled to get dressed, tripping over her own feet.

"Ten seconds," his muffled voice sounded through the

door.

She'd just pulled her last boot on when the door opened.

"Open the other door."

"Other door?" Emily looked around. "There's only mirrors in here."

He shimmied himself inside the cubicle. "That one in front of you. Press it." He pointed to the right side of the center mirror.

In disbelief, Emily did as she was told.

"What about these sensor things?" Emily lifted a security tag that was fixed to her new shirt.

"Quick." He gestured for her to step through the secret door and into a dark passage. "I'll get that sorted shortly. We need to get out of here. Now."

"I'm not even going to ask how you know your way around here."

"It's good to have contacts in this city. Let's get moving."

She looked around. They were back in a passage very similar to the one they'd been in only a few moments ago. Shaking her head, she followed him.

"When we step outside that door," he pointed to a door at the end of the passageway as they walked towards it, "we need to act normal. It's important we blend in. Okay?"

Emily nodded.

"Now, for those tags," he said, stopping.

Emily watched him pull something out of his bag. He grabbed the tag on her shirt and placed the device over it. She kept her eyes on the department store door, waiting for guards or police to walk out, their guns pointed at them.

A bit of tugging and the base of the tag came away. Pulling the pinned tag top out from the shirt, he threw both parts into his bag. Her heart racing — they'd been stationary for too long — Emily helped him locate the other tags.

Pulling the last one away, she re-arranged her clothes so they were sitting right. Her shoulders felt a little lighter with the security burden removed.

Despite that, she still had an awful knot in her tummy. She grabbed her stomach.

"You all right?" he asked.

"I'm not too sure about," she nodded towards their exit, "out there."

"You're right. We're not safe yet. Not by a long shot. Pull your shit together. I can't have you falling apart on me."

"Great." Emily pulled her shoulders back and tried to ignore the knots in her stomach. Putting one foot in front of the other, she walked towards the door that now seemed so far away.

"You ready?" he asked, his hand on the handle.

Emily went to nod but stopped. "Before we go out there... please tell me your name."

"Is it really that important to you?"

"I'm Emily." She extended her hand. "Emily Lee."

"Brian."

He shook her hand.

"Just Brian? Brian no last name?"

He blushed.

"It's okay, Brian Chalmers." She winked at him.

"How did-"

"Come on. Let's get this show on the road." She pushed her hand down on his and opened the door.

The hustle and bustle of city life greeted them. Trams were dinging, arrogant drivers were blaring their car horns, and truck brakes were screeching.

"Anyhow..." She looked over her shoulder. Brian was only just stepping through the door. "It's written on the cover of your folder."

He pulled the folder around, exposing a personalized name label barely five centimeters by two.

"How could you read that?"

"Come on." She gave his arm a tug. "Didn't you say we need to blend in?"

Emily merged with the foot traffic. Brian hurried up to her side.

"So, where are we going?" Emily asked.

"You're going back to school. University, actually."

She stopped. People bumped into her, shoving her as they tried to get past.

"I've done my sentence. I am not going back." She waved her hands in front of her.

Brian grabbed her arm and pulled her along the footpath. His grip was too strong; she had no choice but to follow.

"I'm beginning to think you want to die today," he muttered as she kept pace with him.

"Absolutely not. I've still got places to see and things to do before I die."

"At Uni, we've got access to a secluded basement-"

"Hey, hang on. We've only just met. I'm not ready to go into any basement with you."

He tightened his grip around her arm. Emily tried to pull away but he didn't flinch, his grip tightening still.

He continued as if never interrupted, "With computers and high security. We just need to get there. Alive and unnoticed."

"Why do we need computers? We just need to call the police. I've got a friend in the force. He'll be able to help me. If I don't make contact, his colleagues will be hunting me down when they assume I killed my sister and niece."

"Is that how you got that blood on your clothes?"

Emily looked up at him. Her head barely reached his shoulders. He kept looking ahead, and she followed his lead.

"Yes. But I had nothing to do with it. My apartment was attacked."

"It's okay. I believe you."

"You do?"

"I can't say too much. You don't know who's watching."

He moved his head up only slightly. She followed his gaze. Above them, a security camera was positioned on the side of a building.

Once past it, Brian said, "You're in deep. Possibly too deep."

Chapter 10

Fu inhaled the smell of new leather as he leant back into his leather seat. He sat with his back to his driver while a limp and bloodied Tao sat opposite him, propped up by Fu's two security guards.

As per Fu's standard travel demands, all the curtains in the passenger area were closed except for the one next to him. He liked being aware of his surroundings at any given time, even if he were seeing it backwards.

Heads turned towards them as they traveled by in his stretch limousine. Nothing new.

They approached the last set of traffic lights out of the city and slowed to a stop. Fu's body tensed, his fists clenched. He leaned forward in his chair and looked out his window.

His attention was drawn to a hooded person jaywalking across the street towards them. Fu looked around at the other windows but, as requested, they were all closed.

Looking back out his window, he was able to distinguish it was a young male in his twenties. The man had his eyes fixed right on Fu, as if he was able to see through the heavily tinted windows.

Keeping his eyes on the man, Fu tapped the privacy screen. The panel rolled down to about half way.

"Yes, sir," the driver asked.

Still looking out of his window, Fu was certain the man was pointing something at him.

"Company, right side. Now," Fu yelled.

His security guards moved to the edge of their seat. Tao fell behind them. The stranger had a gun aimed at Fu. His guards drew their guns.

"Boss, wind your window down," the guard closest to the window asked, his gun aimed at the approaching shooter.

The man had stopped in the middle of the tram line, his gun aimed at Fu. Fu slid down his seat until his head was below the window line.

The driver accelerated. Fu heard car horns and brakes squealing all around them.

As the driver rounded the corner, Fu sat up in his seat. Resting his head on his headrest, he closed his eyes. They were now on the homestretch out of the city.

Fu's rest was interrupted by moans from Tao as he began to regain consciousness. Opening an eye, Fu saw Tao had started moving. Closing his eyes, he flicked his fingers towards Tao. Everything was silent again.

"He's too strong-willed for his own good," Fu muttered.

The two guards sniggered but stopped as soon as Fu cracked open an eye and looked at them.

"What are we going to do with him?" the taller and more buff one asked.

"We'll see. A lot can happen between now and then."

Fu's phone rang through his vehicle's Bluetooth system.

"There goes my rest," he said as he accepted the call and took his phone off the limousine's Bluetooth.

"Yeah."

"The girl. She's still alive," a deep male voice said.

"Frick. Casualties?"

"Minimal."

"Good. Time this city woke up a little. Is the package still active?"

"Yes."

"Good. Good." Fu leant back in his chair and thought for a moment before continuing, "Kill her at any cost. Understood? At any cost."

"Yes, sir. At any cost."

Chapter 11

"Don't look behind you," Brian said. "We're being followed."

"Are we far from the University?"

"We're not going to get there in time. Time for Plan B."

"And that is?"

"No idea. Haven't thought that far ahead."

"What are they teaching at University now? You should always have a backup plan. You know. Just in case the first one goes belly up."

They started to cross the road. A tram chimed its bell. Emily looked over. The last of the passengers was boarding.

"This way." She pulled Brian towards the tram.

"This is a bad idea."

"Run."

The tram started to move. She flagged it down. The driver stopped and opened the doors.

"Quick."

Emily ran ahead to the open door and jumped on. Brian wasn't far behind. She looked back towards the foot traffic. A heavy-set man, black jacket, shaven head, was forcing his way through the pedestrians. Brian jumped on board.

"Quick, shut the door. Get moving," she ordered the tram driver.

She looked behind her. The doors slowly closed and the tram began to move. The man's steps had lengthened and he was closing in on them. He picked up his pace as the tram gained momentum. The tram was beginning to pull away from him. A city block away now, and gaining.

They took a seat near the front door. A few passengers, mainly those dressed in business attire, obviously disgruntled at their tram being held up, stared at them. Emily smiled back. The passengers quickly turned away.

"That was close," Emily whispered to Brian.

"Ugh, too close," Brian said.

Emily followed his line of sight out the rear window of the tram. There he stood, on the tram line, with another muscly man. The thugs stood within arm's reach of each other.

"No, not again." She held onto a nearby railing.

"Hold on, everyone," Brian yelled.

Chapter 12

Harry peered out the office window and down the ten floors towards the city street. Police cars were barricading the neighboring intersection while officers were rolling out police tape from one side of the street to the other.

People were running out of neighboring buildings, and armed officers were guiding them down the street, away from his building.

"What's your name?" Harry turned. "You should see these guys. You'd think I have a bloody big bomb or somethin' up here!" Harry sneered.

"It's... it's Sharon," a frightened Sharon Hann responded, looking down at the floor.

She wriggled her wrists but they weren't moving. They

were tied securely to her office chair arm rest.

"Shut up," he yelled. "I don't care what your name is. All I know is that you're screwing the boss instead of keeping the bastard honest."

Sharon looked up. Her mouth dropped open.

"I came here just the other week. I spent all morning driving here, not that you people cared. All I wanted was to get this shit sorted out. It wasn't even bloody lunch when I knocked on his office door. The door was ajar so I peered inside and called out again when I'd seen you two, butt naked, screwin' each other like a pair of bloody rabbits. Not a care in the world."

Harry waved his gun in the air.

"Your boss," he continued. "He waved me off while his face was still shoved in your hair. In between groans, he told me to come back later. So. Here I am. I'm back."

"You shouldn't have. There's other ways to deal with what you're going through. Instead... instead of like this." Sharon looked at the gun still in his hand.

"You reckon, do you? You won't even answer my calls. My emails. You won't even answer my wife or my lawyer. Nothin'."

"We didn't have any messages from you. We didn't know you tried contacting us."

Sharon wiggled in her restraints. They weren't budging.

"Bloody oath, there was. We left them all with you!" Harry snapped. He pointed the gun at Sharon's head. "You personally. Remember, you gave us your direct line when this place took over our mortgage from our previous provider. Remember? Seriously! Do you think I came down in the last shower or somethin'? I may be from the sticks, and you city folk often refer to us as being slow. But I'm far from it. It's snobs like you who often forget we're business owners as well as providers for this country. As business operators, we need to keep ahead of the game just as much as you all do here, in this cement jungle. It must be hard to come to work, what with your climate-controlled buildings and everythin'. You wouldn't last an hour at my workplace."

"Let me get Andrew in here. We can get this all sorted then we can all go home to our families," Sharon suggested.

"You know what? I've got a better idea."

"What's that?"

Harry walked over to Sharon and stood behind her. He pressed the cold metal gun barrel against the back of her head.

"I'll finish you off right now. Then I'll go find Andrew and deal with him, too."

"What will that solve? Nothing."

"No. You are right," Harry said. He lowered the gun and thought for a moment, walking around to face Sharon.

"You're going to help me, for a change."

"Like hell I am!" Her eyes narrowed.

"If you don't, you'll get one of these." Harry threw a bullet. It landed on her lap. "How about you keep that one safe for me? That bullet is reserved just for you."

"YOU BASTARD!" Sharon spat at him.

Chapter 13

The passengers on the tram followed Emily's gaze. Chaos erupted as everyone grabbed onto any part of the tram they could.

Emily looked around. Her stomach dropped. Half way up, a mother sat, whimpering as she huddled her infant child.

Emily rushed to her side. "Please move up this way. Now. Take my seat."

The woman looked up, her eyes puffy and red.

"Thank you," she mouthed.

Emily watched as the mother scurried towards the front. She quickly glanced out the back window. A flare appeared in front of the shooter. She ran towards the front of the tram.

"Duck," she heard Brian yell out.

The mother was just in front of her. They were still a couple of seats away from the very front of the tram. Launching herself in the air, Emily pulled the woman and child down with her and huddled her body over theirs.

A loud explosion erupted. The tram rocked from the impact.

Emily heard the mother praying, kissing her child's head.

"It's going to be okay. They're after me, not you," Emily told the woman.

The rear end of the tram lifted.

"Hold on," she whispered into the mother's ear.

Grabbing a chair leg with her free arm, she held onto the woman and infant.

The tram lifted higher. The mother was slipping out of her grasp. Locking her arm around the chair leg, Emily gritted her teeth. Using all the strength in her other arm, she held onto the woman and infant.

As the tram continued to rise, they began to slide. Grip tight, arm locked, Emily pulled the mother and child closer to the chair.

She glanced over at Brian.

"Hold on, Brian," she yelled.

He was holding onto a support railing with both hands, and his feet were up against the side of the tram, his body braced between the two.

Brian looked up and winked at her before returning his concentration to stopping his body from becoming a human cannon ball.

Looking around, Emily watched on as passengers were being thrown towards the front of the tram, their screams trailing behind them.

She felt the tram's incline slow down, until it stopped.

"Get ready," Emily yelled.

The tram tilted to its side.

She heard an older man yell, "Move to the other side."

Before anyone had a chance to move, the tram tipped and crashed on its side. The sound of shattering glass and metal colliding with steel tracks echoed through the tram.

Emily was slammed against the chairs before coming to a stop across a couple of chair legs.

Her chest felt heavy. She lay there in a daze, rubbing her head. Numb. The mother and infant were lying on top of her.

Emily stirred when she heard glass shattering nearby. Looking around, she quickly spotted Brian kicking the front window out.

Emily went to get up but couldn't. She was pinned down.

"Ma'am." Emily shook the woman on top of her. "Ma'am!"

The woman's infant started crying.

"Ma'am, wake up." She shook her again. No reaction. "Brian," Emily yelled while trying to stir the mother.

"What's up?"

"She's not responding. She's not allowed to die. She has a baby to bring up."

Brian felt the woman's pulse and shook his head. "There's a very feint pulse."

"No!" Emily shook her head.

She tried to move the woman but only managed to free one of her arms.

Brian handed her the crying infant.

"I, I don't want this." Emily tried handing the infant back.

"Get over yourself. We need to get the mother out of here. Now," he said as he lifted the mother up. "You there," Brian yelled at a passenger.

Emily craned her neck around to see a woman in her late fifties turn around.

"You okay?" Brian asked.

She nodded. "I think so. Just a few bumps and scratches."

"Please look after the infant." He nodded his head towards Emily. "Stay with the mother until the paramedics get here. Please."

The woman nodded again and maneuvering over the carnage reached Emily.

"Is this your sweet child?" the woman asked.

Emily tried to force a smile but a tear rolled down her face. "No. Her mother is being carried out right now."

"Oh, poor child," the woman said as she picked up the infant. "It's going to be okay." She tapped the infant's bottom and the crying subsided.

"Wow," Emily said.

"Grandma's touch." She winked at Emily. "You did a wonderful thing protecting this precious child and her mother."

"Thank you. But we need to get out of here." Emily smiled.

The woman clambered out of the tram, tottering on her

legs as she held a protective arm over the infant.

Emily moved her legs around until she felt the wall of the tram. She shuffled her body down until she was crouching in between the two seats.

"Are you all right to get up?" Brian asked as he re-entered the tram.

"Just working that out now," Emily said as she tried to stand. "Ouch," she grimaced as she applied pressure on her foot. Putting her weight on her other leg, she looked down. The ankle appeared to be swollen.

Brian grabbed her arm and did his best to guide her out of the tram. Limping over the shattered windows and the exposed uneven road, she stumbled along and maneuvered over the front dash, grabbing the side window frame on her way through.

Pain sliced through her hand and wrist as she pulled herself through.

"Shoot," she said, applying pressure to her wrist.

Blood was dripping from the wound.

"Don't touch." Brian pulled her arm away. "Let me have a look."

He held her hand and inspected the wound.

"I'll be all right." Emily pulled her hand away. "It's just a surface wound."

"Looks deep. We need to get it looked at."

"Right after I get away from that man." She pointed down the street.

"Here, put this around it." Brian pulled a gauze pad and

bandage roll from his backpack.

"Thank you."

Emily wrapped her hand. Inspecting her medic handiwork, she turned to show Brian. He wasn't there.

"Brian?" she asked, looking around.

She received a few shrugs from other badly wounded passengers.

Then there was movement. Brian staggered out with another person supported over his shoulder. She took a closer look and recognized the man on Brian's shoulder.

"The driver," she yelled.

Cheers and applause erupted around her.

Ignoring the pain in her ankle, Emily limped over. "Here." She placed her body under the tram driver's arm and helped Brian get him away from the wreckage.

The applause became louder as they seated the tram driver amongst the passengers. A few patted Brian on the back, thanking him.

Brian shrugged it off. "It's okay. Just doing my good deed."

Nearby pedestrians were running over to assist, offering water, jackets and shirts, anything they had on them to help compress the passengers' wounds.

Emily gently pulled Brian away from the crowd.

"Can we go now?"

Brian looked up and down the road. "Is the gunman still around?"

Chapter 14

Limping to the upturned tram, Emily peered around the corner and down the tram line. The line was empty.

"No, but he won't be too far away." She looked around the street and along the footpaths trying to spot him.

"You okay to walk?" Brian asked.

"Gingerly, yeah. I'll be fine."

"This way."

Everyone was busy attending to the passengers while more passersby stopped to render assistance. Slipping past the crowd, they took one more look around them before stepping into a nearby alleyway.

"We've got to stop going into alleys."

"You were right. You'll be just fine. There's nothing wrong

with your humor."

"How far to the Uni?" Emily asked, half skipping to keep up with Brian's fast pace.

"Change of plan. There's too much heat on us. You've pissed off someone today. We need to go underground. And soon."

"Underground? For how long?"

"As long as it takes to find out what is going on."

"Better not be too long. My father... he's not well."

"How long's a piece of string?"

Emily stopped and stared at him.

"Look, I'm sorry. I honestly don't know. I'm putting my own neck on the line here trying to help keep you alive."

"I'm sorry. I am grateful for your help."

They continued walking.

"It's almost like," Emily shrugged, "you were meant to be there today."

Brian kept walking, his head bent over, focused on his cell phone's screen, no hesitation in his pace.

"You all right there?" Emily asked nodding to his phone.

Brian's shoulders flexed. "Ah, yeah, sorry. Just trying to find somewhere to bunk down."

"Any luck?"

"We'll soon find out."

They stopped at a corner. Emily poked her head around the building. Their alleyway spilled into a major street. People everywhere, all too busy getting to their destination to worry about a couple of strangers standing on an alley corner.

She scanned the crowd. "All clear," she said.

"Right. Remember we need to blend in with the traffic."

Emily took one last look around and fell in with the next flow of pedestrians, bracing every step, trying to ensure she was walking as normally as possible.

Brian stepped into line with Emily.

"If we get separated you need to follow this street down to Little Bourke St. Follow the street up until you reach Chinatown."

"I can't. I'm not allowed in there."

"You will continue along until you find a shop called Lo Lang's Dumplings. Ask for Li Jun Zhang. He'll look after you."

"Look after me?"

He tapped on his cell phone screen. A moment later her phone beeped.

"The co-ordinates are on your phone."

She looked at her phone and then back at Brian, confused.

"How did you-"

"It's my job. You do know they're not as secure as you're led to believe."

"This has high security on it."

"You sure about that?" He raised an eyebrow. "All I can say is that the phone developers have conducted some pretty smart marketing to convince you and the general user population their phones are secure."

Brian looked over his shoulder, and Emily followed his gaze.

"Can you walk a little faster?"

"Why? There's no one following us." She looked over her shoulder again.

Everyone was moving in sync with each other. She received a few disgruntled looks from the men walking behind her. Besides those couple of men, she couldn't see anyone sticking out or looking directly at them.

"Trust me, there is. Two men. Broad shoulders. Large biceps. Black skin-tight t-shirts. About a dozen people back."

Chapter 15

Harry walked back over to the window. Looking skyward, he collected his thoughts.

"There's a video recording you have." He turned to face Sharon. "It has my family and me on it. You're going to get it for me."

"What on earth do you want with it? It's evidence."

"We're going to get some bloody popcorn and ice cream. Then we're going to watch it. Together."

"You already know what happened."

"Get it. And seein' how young and naive you are, I'm going to show you what type of company you're working for," Harry said.

He untied one of her hands from the chair and pushed the

phone closer to Sharon. She paused for a moment. Harry raised his gun to her head. She punched in a couple of numbers.

Three rings came through the telephone's speaker.

"Nobody's here. They've all probably been evac-"

"H...Hello," a cautious voice on the end said.

Harry believed the owner of the voice was young, and this was probably one of her first jobs out of school.

"It's Sharon Hann here. Can you get the recent video of client Harry Fry?"

"Uh... but I-" the nervous voice responded.

"Email it through to this computer," Harry said, waving his gun at Sharon's computer.

"It's still... in the backlog of being uploaded to our services."

"I don't bloody care. Get it sent through to this computer."

Harry fired the gun into the roof. Sharon squealed.

"Do it. Now. Or the next one will go in Sharon's head," Harry demanded.

"Okay... okay. I'll do it next."

"You'll do it now."

Harry picked up the hand receiver and slammed it down.

"What do we do now?" Sharon asked.

"We sit in a circle and sing Kumbaya." Harry shook his head. "What do you think? We wait, and you'd better pray to whoever it is you pray to that the video appears on that computer before I get bored of waitin'."

Harry paced back and forth from the office door to the

window, checking out the door into the hallway and the street outside. Each time, he noted there hadn't been any new movements. Harry was growing anxious. He quickened his pacing.

A ding echoed through the room.

"What was that?" Harry demanded. He swung around with his gun aimed at Sharon.

"It's okay," Sharon said. "It's just something coming through on the computer."

"It had better be that damn video."

Harry stood behind Sharon and watched as she opened the bank's internal messaging service.

"See here," she pointed to the bold line of text indicating the details of the email. "One new message."

She clicked on the email.

"That's no video. It's a single of line of jumbled-up words. Where is it?"

"It's attached behind this hyperlink."

"Hyper what? Never mind. Just load it."

Sharon clicked on the link. "Hope this was all worth it."

"You'd better believe it will be. I'm going to get back what you stole from my family, and you're going to help me."

Chapter 16

They were half way down the city block. Emily pretended to look at something across the road and shot a glance from the corner of her eye towards the rear of the crowd.

That was strange. Maybe the men had just disappeared and weren't following them at all. But why would Brian lie to her? Brian's been actively trying to save my life so far, hasn't he? He was on his way to Uni. He could've just disappeared with the scurries of people. Instead, he pulled me to safety.

Emily turned to Brian. He was focused. Almost military-like. Shoulders pulled back, head straight, and no emotion on his face.

Unlocking her phone, she looked at the co-ordinates Brian had sent earlier. Chinatown. She recalled the last time she was in a Chinatown community. The time she was forbidden from entering any other Chinese community, worldwide.

It had happened one month ago. She was at a trendy bar in Sydney's Chinatown, enjoying the music and a drink at the bar with a colleague. Showing him a glimpse of her culture while they were quietly celebrating the successful sting, the successful arrest of a Chinese crime boss who'd been untouchable for the last five years.

The Australian Federal Police had called on her services to assist them with a case they'd been working on and for which they needed an insider. Someone who was trusted and respected in the community and who would give them the edge to make a case against the villain finally stick.

Emily and her colleague were getting up from the bar when a fight between two Chinese gangs erupted nearby. Edging towards the door, she was dragged into the fight, kicked and beaten until she couldn't move. She remembered trying to fight back, being successful at the beginning but being soon outnumbered.

After blacking out, she woke up in a hospital bed, her frail father looking over her. She hadn't forgotten the look of pain on his face.

His final words to her were etched in her memory: "You have betrayed our family, your mother, myself. We, along with all Chinese communities, disown you. You are no longer one of us."

That had been the last time she'd seen him.

Emily felt her arm being pulled. She returned to the

bustling streets of inner Melbourne. Her foot extended out over the road. A red man was flashing on the pedestrian traffic light. A driver honked their car horn. Emily looked up and saw a car approaching. She pulled her foot back from the road as the car sped past.

"Focus," Brian said. "They're still following us. Back a bit farther than earlier and across the road."

Emily moved from foot to foot. The red flashing man looked down at her. She glanced down both sides of the road. Nothing. Finally, she stepped out onto the road as the man changed to green.

"Thank you," Emily said.

Brian didn't answer.

She stopped a few steps onto the road, the swarm of pedestrians pushing her around, and turned to her side. Brian wasn't there. She looked behind her, to the curb. Two men were holding Brian back.

He wriggled to get free but the men holding him held their ground.

"Get out of here," he yelled. "Now."

One of the men hit Brian across the back of the head with the butt of a gun. Brian's head flopped over.

Chapter 17

Emily looked around, then across the street. She spotted two men, both with similar appearances, looking in her direction.

Turning around, she broke into a run, pushing through the very people who were in a rush to get around her. She glanced over her shoulder and saw the men crossing the busy intersection. Car tires squealed and horns blared as the men continued to disrupt the flow of traffic.

Nearly across the street, she saw the red pedestrian man flashing in front of her. *Give a girl some time to cross the road, will ya!* she thought as she continued to run.

To her left, a noise caught her attention, a heavy engine. She turned to see a medium rigid truck accelerating as it approached the intersection. There was nothing between her and the truck, and it wasn't showing any signs of slowing down.

With one hard push, she stepped onto the curb as the truck sped past her, ploughing into the build-up of cars already held up across the intersection by the men following her.

She kept running, keeping a tab on her surroundings – street signs, cars, people, dogs, anything and everything.

Behind her she heard women screaming, men yelling abuse and glassware smashing. Not turning around, she kept pushing forward, knowing all too well who was causing the commotion.

Reaching another intersection, she glanced up at the sign. It read, Bourke Street.

Not waiting for any flashing red men to turn green and indicate it was safe to cross, she made her way across the intersection, dodging cars and tapping on bonnets who merely missed her.

The footsteps behind became louder. Pushing people out of the way, Emily stepped out onto the road, running against the traffic, ignoring the car horns as she kept running.

Looking over her shoulder, she saw the men were still chasing her but one of them was struggling with her pace. This was causing cars to stop before they could try to maneuver around them while at the same time trying to avoid hitting other vehicles.

"Suckers," she whispered.

Putting more effort into her stride, she began to put some distance between them and her.

The next intersection was narrower than the previous one. One-way traffic. Across the street, she read, Little Bourke Street on the sign.

Chinatown.

Turning around, she saw the men were still running towards her, guns now visible in their hands.

"Shit."

She paused at the intersection and looked back down Little Bourke Street. There were lots of people and cars moving about.

The men were still closing in, both now running.

She shook her head. No, she couldn't run into Chinatown. Not now. If she was going to step back in there, she needed to be able to slip back into the community unnoticed. There was no way she could do that with men chasing her. She'd probably also have half of Chinatown chasing after her next.

She moved away from the intersection, taking one last look down Little Bourke Street before she broke back into a run.

Need a Plan C, and now, she told herself.

Emily kept running up the road, along the dotted line that separated the lanes of traffic.

She noticed the volume of traffic increasing as she ran. Her elbow room was diminishing to the point that cars and trucks were swerving out of her way. Behind her she heard plastic and metal crumpling as vehicles collided with each other. Not looking back, she pushed on.

She heard more yelling from frustrated drivers and knew her followers weren't far behind her.

In between her feet connecting with the asphalt, she flicked through the contacts on her cell phone until she found the name she was looking for and dialed the number.

The phone rang. She switched the call to her phone's speakers.

"Schultz," a male's voice answered at the other end.

"Oh, good. You answered," Emily said in between deep breaths.

"Emily?"

"Yes. I think I'm in some deep stuff."

"You back in town?"

"You can kinda say that."

"I'm tied up in a case right now." His voice lowered. "How about we meet down at our bar, say at four o'clock?"

"Was kinda hoping for earlier?"

"It's not even lunch time yet." He chuckled.

"I'm being serious. Some crazy stuff," she took a deep breath, "has been going down today."

"Tell me about it. The hostage situation, multiple murders and a derailed tram. We're all working double time. Even calling everyone in that's on leave or day off."

"Yeah. About that."

"You sound like you're running. Being back in town making you wanting to break out the sneakers?"

"Funny. Now focus."

"Right. Sorry."

"I think I may be in a little bit of trouble."

"Little?"

"Okay, maybe more than a little."

Emily stepped off the road and onto the footpath. Pedestrians dodged out of her way.

"There's someone, some people, who I have a sneaky suspicion might be trying to kill me."

"Are you sure? Maybe you've been in the wrong place at the wrong time."

Silence. Emily felt anger brewing up inside her. She thumped a street sign as she ran past it.

"A gunman, in a corridor, shooting directly at me."

"Fair point."

"How about an RPG targeted at the tram I'd just hopped in?"

"Coincidence."

Gunshots.

"Shit." Emily raised her hand over her head.

More shots followed.

A street sign next to her pinged. She looked up and saw a bullet lodged in it. She continued to put one foot in front of the other.

Around her, people were screaming and scurrying everywhere. The chaos was making it difficult for Emily to get away.

More gunfire.

This time she felt something hit her shoulder. While still running, she pulled her shirt collar down. She felt around the wound but couldn't feel anything solid in her shoulder.

"What's wrong? What's going on?" Schultz asked.

Emily ran back out onto the road, weaving in between the traffic.

"Ah, just ducking some friendly gunfire," she replied.

The gunfire followed her. Their shots were off, connecting with everything but her. She paused behind a parked tram.

"You call this a coincidence?" Emily asked.

"Where are you? I'll send some uniforms to get you out of there."

"No, it'll be what they want. More police tied up. Who knows what else they've got planned in town today?"

Emily risked a glance back. The men were closing.

She needed to move.

An old truck pulled up next to her.

Crouching, she maneuvered around the truck to the passenger side.

She stepped up the steps and opened the passenger door.

"Afternoon." She nodded at the driver as she sat in and closed the door.

He looked at her, his mouth hanging open. She could see his mouth moving but there were no noises coming out.

"Light's green." Emily pointed at the traffic light.

"Oh. Yep." The driver shook his head as he started to slowly shift through the numerous gears. "I don't have anything of value in here, or at home. I'm just a worker. A hard one at that."

Emily chuckled.

"I'm not here to hurt you. I'm after a favor," she said.

"Right." The driver looked at her out of the corner of his

eye.

"Where are you?" Schultz asked.

Emily ignored him.

"See those men back there?" she asked the driver.

The driver looked at his side mirror and replied, "Yeah."

"I need to get away from them."

"I'm heading to Footscray. That's as far as I can get you."

Emily thought for a second.

"I need to call you back," she told Schultz and disconnected the phone call.

Chapter 18

Emily flicked through her notifications until she found the one with the co-ordinates Brian had sent her. She noticed what looked like a quaint garden area at one end of Chinatown.

"Can you take me to Spring Street?" she asked the driver.

The truck driver thought about it for a moment while he continued to change through the gears.

"Where 'bout?"

"Spring Street, corner of Spring and Little Bourke. Right here."

Emily pointed to the intersection. The driver squinted and shrugged.

"It's on the other side of the city."

"Can you take me there or not?" she asked.

"Because you asked so nicely, I will. Just don't get any blood on my seat. Don't want to have to explain that one to the boss."

He flipped on the indicator switch and turned into a quieter street. Black smoke puffed out of the exhaust as he put his foot down on the accelerator pedal.

"Thank you." Emily coughed the fumes out of her lungs.

"Sorry 'bout that. She's a little tired," he rubbed his dash for good luck. "But she still gets the job done. We've been together longer than the wife and I. Pretty much a second marriage."

She smiled and kept an eye on the map on her phone and her surroundings, regularly checking her side mirror, making sure they were alone.

Being careful to keep her shoulder away from the back rest, she sat back in her seat and breathed out a huge sigh of relief.

"What's a young lass like you doing, getting yourself into trouble?"

"When I know, I'll let you know."

"Bad day?"

"Something like that."

"There's been a bit of that happening in the city today."

"I've heard."

"It's been crazy trying to get around the city. What with all the road closures and detours. You can't just take this old girl down any street, you know."

Emily zoned out from his ramblings and watched as the

city streets passed by.

The driver made some more turns and the traffic built up again. At least it was flowing here.

Emily kept a constant eye on her side mirror, watching for any suspicious movement from the vehicles behind them. Nothing. Not of any importance, anyway.

"Here we go, ma'am," the driver announced as he pulled his truck into a parking spot marked as a loading zone.

Emily looked out her window. An illuminated sign positioned above glass sliding doors read "201 Park Tower." A modest entrance. Nothing screaming 'look at me'. Hudsons Coffee next door.

I could really do with a coffee, Emily thought.

She looked out the driver's window and saw what closely resembled a Chinese garden. Well, the city's attempt at replicating an oriental garden.

Looking around the garden, she noticed it occupied the small space between the two sections of streets.

"Thank you." She shook the driver's hand and disembarked from his truck.

He drove off while she stood on the side of the road, coughing through his black exhaust fumes again.

As the fumes disappeared, she stood there and admired the Chinese lions sitting there looking grand and guarding the steps leading into the gardens. It'd been a long time since she'd seen a Chinese garden. Last time would've been when her step father, Tao, had taken her and her family to his home town to meet his family.

The smell of freshly brewed coffee filtered across from the coffee shop and distracted her from the garden and her memories of China.

She closed her eyes and took a couple of deep breaths in.

"Aussie coffee. How I've missed you," she said to herself.

She received a few strange looks as people busily walked past her, but she didn't care. No one knew her here.

She stepped inside Hudsons Coffee; the overpowering smell of coffee filled the shop and the sound of coffee machines brewing the next elixir made her smile wide.

Emily looked around. A few couples and some business people were seated there. They were either making small talk in between sips or reading newspapers.

A handsome barista stood at the counter, complete with an Aussie tan complexion and a few days' stubble growth, but looking well maintained and with a pleasant smile that fitted perfectly his buff-looking body.

Emily felt her cheeks begin to burn. She returned the smile and stepped over to the counter.

To his side was a smorgasbord of various sandwiches, wraps, savories and sweets.

"Er...," she said, flustered, "espresso, please. Double if you can."

"One of those days?" He nodded to her bloody shoulder.

"You won't believe me."

"Take away or in here?"

Emily looked around the shop then out the front door.

"Take away. Please."

"Can I tempt you with a muffin?" he asked.

Her mouth watered at the sight of all the decadent food.

"Why not? It'll probably be the only thing I'll get to eat for a while. How about a chicken wrap, too, please?"

She handed over a twenty-dollar note and he punched the sale through the till. He held out her change.

"Keep the change." She folded her arms and raised her eyebrow at him.

He placed the change in their tip jar.

"Won't be long," the barista advised, winking as he turned to prepare the order.

Emily glanced outside the shop then back inside.

"I'll be just out the front on one of your tables," she called out to him.

He waved his hand, acknowledging her.

She stepped outside, pulled out a metal outdoor chair and tried to get comfortable. Legs crossed, she kept an eye on her surroundings.

Her phone rang.

She glanced at the caller ID.

"Schultz," she said.

She pressed the accept button.

"Yeah," she said, placing the phone on speaker.

"Emily, where are you?"

"I'm safe. For now. Think I've lost them."

"I need to see you. Now. There's some questions I need to ask you."

"You're talking to me now. Ask away."

"In person. It's serious." His voice was stern.

She sat up and took the phone off speaker.

"How serious? I haven't done anything."

"No, you haven't. Not directly. If I don't talk to you, uniforms will be hunting you down."

"That serious?"

Emily thought for a moment.

"Meet me..." She looked at her watch before continuing. "Ten minutes. Tianjin Gardens. Alone. No plainclothes, no uniforms. Only you. Understood?"

Chapter 19

Today was not a normal day at Fu's newly acquired warehouse. He'd been overseeing the refurbishment, turning it from a run-down, musty old warehouse to a state of the art fish processing plant.

The warehouse had to go through a complete re-vamp over the last week due to a new production line needing to be installed. Plans were in place for a cosmetic makeover of the factory floor and walls to commence next week, after giving his construction workers a well-deserved couple of days off.

It had been many years since the family business had implemented changes like this one. Usually Fu would be signing off on permit applications to tear buildings down and build bigger and newer high-rise buildings in their place, with international investors lining up for a piece of the action before the soil was broken.

Fu was now expanding his family's empire, which would soon be his own, into the south-western areas of Melbourne. With his financial backing, he had the manpower and money to push all other syndicates out of there. In a few short months this whole area would be all his to oversee.

Today, Fu had company in his modest refurbished office. It was cozy, with just enough room for a couple of desks, and it now felt cramped with everyone in here.

Sitting opposite him, his two guards towered over a barely conscious Tao, who was slumped in an office chair. Fu watched on as Tao struggled to hold his head up. His eyes flickered before they focused on Fu.

"What do you want with me?" Tao asked.

"Strength. Willpower. You know. A warrior." Fu circled around his brother, looking down at him like he was a rodent.

"You know I'm a fighter. I used to beat you in battles."

"Are you? Still?"

Tao bowed his head. "No. No, you're the younger and stronger one."

"We cannot have weak people in the company."

"What are you saying?" Tao looked up to his brother.

"Your daughter. That thing you adopted. She's been interfering in our business dealings."

"I... I highly doubt it. She learnt her lesson after Sydney."

"Are you sure about that?"

Tao didn't reply; instead, he looked at Fu in disbelief.

"Brian?" Fu turned to the other desk.

Brian poked his head above the numerous screens that lined that desk.

"Pull up the video of her with Andrew. From, I believe, last fortnight... or was it a month ago? You know the one I'm talking about."

Brian lowered his head behind the screens and tapped away at the keyboard. After a few clicks, Brian turned one of the screens around.

Fu nodded his head to Brian, who clicked the play button.

Fu watched Tao, waiting.

The video started, without sound.

It showed Andrew working on his computer. He looked towards a door, and a young woman, nicely dressed in a suit, walked in. Andrew raised his eyebrow and a mischievous smile appeared on his face. The woman sat down on the chair opposite him and angled her body to the side. Her face was now side-on to the camera. She flung her hair back from her face, tucking the stray pieces behind her ear.

Fu noticed Tao's face drop the moment he recognized the woman.

"Emily." His eyes welled up. "My baby."

"That's right. Andrew informed me your baby was investigating the speed of some recent land transfers."

Tao's eyes were stuck to the screen, his eyes swelling with tears.

"I made some inquiries. She isn't currently assigned to any active cases. No one I spoke to knew she was back in the country."

Fu turned the screen back around.

"Why? What has she got herself into?" Tao asked.

"She's brought unwanted attention to our recent acquisitions. The syndicate are not happy. After today, she's no longer going to be causing us any trouble."

"What do you mean?" The wrinkles on his face deepened. "You're not going to hurt her. Are you?"

"She asked for it. It's about time she learnt the ultimate price for meddling in other people's business."

"No, Fu. No, you can't."

"I'm sorry. Well. No, I'm not," he chuckled. "But orders are already in place. I can't stop now that the wheels are in motion. And by the way, didn't you disown her back in Sydney?"

Tao stood up to look his brother in the eye. Fu stood a little higher than his older brother.

"One phone call," Tao pleaded. "And this can be all called off."

"Unlike you, to beg. I don't go back on my orders."

"I don't know who you are anymore. This," he moved his hand up and down Fu, "is not how we were brought up. Father would be disgusted by what you're becoming."

Fu nodded his head to his guards. They pulled Tao back into his chair and secured his arms to the armrests and his feet to the chair legs.

"It's a good thing he isn't here." Fu spat at Tao's feet.

Tao wriggled in his chair but he wasn't going anywhere.

Fu's phone rang.

"Yeah," he answered.

"Sorry, boss. She... She... uh... got away," a deep male voice spoke on the other end of the line.

"Do I have to come out there and do your job for you? You had one simple task, and you cannot even do that."

There was silence on the other end.

"You'd better find her," Fu continued. "Before I do."

He ended the call and turned to Brian. "Find her."

Brian nodded and stared at the computer screen as his fingers flew over the keyboard.

Tao laughed. "She's too good for your men?"

Fu nodded to his men. They moved in. Their fists flung into Tao's already frail body. Kicks hammered up and down Tao's legs. One kick landed in his stomach and the chair tilted over and fell back with a loud thud. They continued to lay punches into his now unresponsive and bloodied body.

Fu walked past the brawling men. "Play nice with him. I'll be back. With her."

Chapter 20

Emily sipped her coffee while leaning against a mid-height concrete wall positioned at the north end of the garden.

From here she had a full view, from the neighboring balconies to the entire oriental garden, including the steps leading down to Parliament Station.

She checked her watch.

"One more minute and I'm outta here," she murmured.

Looking up, she saw Schultz walking through the garden from the Nicholson Street entrance.

Moving around behind the wall, she stopped behind a tree. Its low hanging branches hid her from view. His rigid posture dominated the relaxed postures of those around him.

Stopping at the steps in between the two lion guards, he

faced the one-lane Spring Street.

Emily scanned her surroundings. A few more people were hovering around the gardens now. Many were by themselves, admiring the statues or reading newspapers.

She watched Schultz while he looked around, following his gaze, ensuring he was alone.

He looked at his wrist. His watch glistened in the sun. As he turned his back to her, she saw him hold his suit sleeve up to his mouth for a few seconds.

Emily noticed a few men respond in. *Well they're not here for the beauty of the gardens.* She unlocked her phone and pulled up her recent call list, dialing Schultz' number.

It rang a couple of times. Schultz moved his leg but kept alert. The call rang out. Emily dialed it again.

"Where are you?" Schultz answered, frustration in his voice.

"I said alone."

"I am."

"You sure? How about the man standing behind you, admiring the pond? Or the one reading the newspaper on the concrete border?"

"Where are you?" He looked around, high and low, searching. "We need to talk. If we don't, these men are the least of your worries."

"With what I've faced today, these boys will be a walk in the park."

Still on the line, she stepped out from behind the concrete wall and under the oriental pergola.

"Slowly, turn around. No sudden movements."

"You're directing orders at an AFP agent?" Yet Schultz slowly turned around.

"You want to talk to me? Yeah? Well, I'm here."

Schultz's gaze swept right over her, his eyes shifting to the traffic over her shoulder. Then his head slowly moved towards her.

He squinted when he first saw her, and then a flash of recognition appeared on his face.

Emily didn't blame him for not recognizing her straight away; after all, she was battered and bruised, wearing her second set of torn clothing and sporting bird's nest hair.

She hung up the phone while Schultz approached but kept her eyes on the other men. Clearly, they were with him. They avoided eye contact and stepped closer, ensuring Schultz was maintaining the same distance from them.

"Emily," Schultz said as he stepped up the concrete steps leading to the pergola Emily was standing under.

She extended her arms for their usual friendly embrace.

"Seat." He pointed to a nearby concrete seat.

Confused, she dropped her arms and sat down.

"This is business," Schultz told her, taking a seat alongside her.

"I... I understand. Sorry. It's just been one of those days."

She looked out to the gardens, trying to forget the humiliating feeling of rejection.

"Do you know this man?" Schultz asked, nudging her shoulder.

Emily turned to see a photo on his cell phone screen. A deceased man. She assumed it was a morgue photo because of the metallic background.

She turned away, to the beauty of the garden.

"Do you recognize him?" Schultz asked again.

Emily cleared a large knot in her throat.

"No. No, I don't. Sorry I can't help you." Emily stood up.

"Not. So. Quick." He tugged her back down to the seat.

"Oi," she snapped, pulling her arm back. "If this is business, I'm outta here."

"Take another look." He shoved the phone in front of her. "Are you positive you don't know him?"

She sat there, staring at the screen, her stomach churning. One side of his head was mangled, like it had connected with something hard.

"I'd hate to have to take you in to complete our questioning."

No, it couldn't be. *I can't have lost him and my sister both on the same day. No one can know.*

"Um, yeah... that's by brother in law. Tom."

Her eyes welled up. My sister's little family. The one she'd longed for since she and Tom were high school sweethearts. All gone. In one day. Life sucks today.

She wiped her eyes. Schultz sat in silence. Out of the corner of her eye she could see him watching her. She shuffled on the seat, avoiding eye contact with him.

"Where was he found?"

"In the alleyway. Behind your apartment."

"My apartment?" Emily asked.

"Where your sister and niece were found. Deceased."

She fought back the tears.

"Where were you?"

"With her. I know this looks bad." She placed her hand on his knee but he pushed it away. Emily was taken aback but quickly continued, "That apartment was shot at."

"How come you didn't report it? Or call me?"

"I tried. The phone was blocked. I couldn't call out."

"Right. I think you need to come with me."

"I'm telling you the truth. You know me. I can't lie."

"Your phone has been working since. Why didn't you tell me on any of the phone calls we've had since?"

"I kinda was trying to save my own life."

"Very well." Schultz paused, thinking. "The ammunition found in your apartment matches the ammunition that was found in his gun."

A gun. Since when did he have a gun? He hadn't had one since he'd been discharged from the Army.

Schultz continued. "Is there any reason why he would want to kill his wife? Your sister?"

Emily shrugged her shoulders. Her mind drifted to the last time she was with him. In his arms, their naked bodies barely touching. His gentle touch, his embrace.

"He loved Soph very much."

"Was your sister happy in her marriage?"

"Of course she was. Yeah, she was tired, looking after her daughter and our father. But she doted over Tom."

"Was Tom aware you were back in town?"

"No. Only you and Soph knew."

Schultz studied her before continuing. "Any reason why you'd be a target, then?"

Emily shook her head.

"Any disgruntled clients? Death threats?"

Emily thought. She was always hopping between locations, relocating to wherever the next client was.

"No. No, there haven't been any. All my mail gets redirected into my email inbox. There's been nothing come through on that, or my cell."

Emily thought for a moment. There could be multiple reasons why someone would target her. It could even be repercussions from her informant situation in Sydney last month. Or even one of her many assignments where she'd been employed by companies to uncover dodgy members of staff who were money laundering their bosses' turnover."

"What's your current project?"

"Ugh, what's that got to do with anything?"

"We need to get a full picture of what on earth is going on here. Melbourne has never seen so much mayhem. Let alone all on the same day."

"Sorry. Just on edge with what's happened today. But no, I'm about to start a new project later this week. After spending a relaxing couple of weeks soaking in a Caribbean Island culture. I arrived here early to settle in and catch up with a few people before I started."

"Nice," he said, clearly envious. "Before that, what were you working on?"

"Just a quick bookkeeping job for a friend."

"Bookkeeping?" Schultz raised an eyebrow. "Little below your pay grade."

Emily chuckled. "I owed a friend a favor. Just helped them out for a few days while they found a new bookkeeper. And it helped get back into sync with the grass root fundamentals of accounting. After all, it's what businesses are based on, aren't they?"

Schultz looked at his cell phone then out to the garden. He seemed to be contemplating his next move. How to word it properly. Emily began to feel ill at ease as she watched him.

The detective standing at the base of the steps leading to the pergola stepped closer.

Emily shifted in her seat. She wiped her hot and clammy hands down her jeans.

"Okay, then." Schultz looked down at his phone. "Explain this. A new project of yours?" He showed her a photo.

Chapter 21

Emily tried to grab the phone from Schultz, but he kept it just out of arm's reach.

"Can I zoom in? It's too small."

"You don't recognize it at all?"

She squinted, to show him she was studying the photo. But she'd already recognized it. The shades of black, white and gray were her apartment wall. A knot had developed in her stomach, twisting and turning.

While keeping a straight face, she replied, "Oh, that." She waved it off. "Nothing big. It's just a little side project I've been working on for the last few months. You know, to keep my research skills fresh in between jobs."

"Looks like a little more than a side project."

"You know me," she shrugged. "Always learning. Always researching something trivial."

"Only this," Schultz waved his phone, "isn't trivial. Is it?"

Emily looked away. She couldn't look at him. They'd worked on many projects together. But she'd never seen the hurt on his face like he was showing now. It was like looking at the hurt on her father's face when he'd learnt she'd betrayed him and his Chinese community.

"Our forensic team have started looking into your research." Schultz continued. "They've advised me you're in deep."

"Don't know why. It's just your normal, straightforward unethical banking behavior. The boss is a conniving sleaze. He doesn't care whom he destroys while he climbs the corporate ladder."

"There's more to this investigation than you're telling me."

"Not sure what you mean. I was following up on the increased media attention to the unethical banking behavior in the banking sector."

"Do you know who has been trying to kill you today?"

"No idea. Right from the get-go, I've been targeted. They've shot at my apartment, and they shot at me ever since I left it after my sister was killed. If Brian hadn't helped me get away, I'd be dead, as well."

"Brian?" Schultz asked.

"Yeah. Brian. Brian Chalmers."

"Brian Chalmers?"

On edge, Emily looked around her, up and down the street.

Ensuring the hunters hadn't caught up with her.

A man similarly suited to Schultz approached from the Nicholson Street side.

Emily eyed the man up and down, her eyes narrowed. Her legs automatically positioned themselves to flee if needed.

He flashed his badge.

Emily relaxed a little but kept her eye on him as he whispered into Schultz's ear.

Schultz's eyes saddened as he turned to face Emily.

"Emily," Schultz said. "We need to take you into protective custody."

On her feet, she waved her hands in front of her. "I am not going down that track. I've worked too damn hard to get my career to where it is today."

"You're in grave danger. You thought Sydney was bad. This will be nothing if they get their hands on you."

"I... I don't understand." Emily placed her hands on her hips.

"Check your phone," the detective advised Schultz.

Schultz clicked on the notification and showed Emily another photo.

Her mouth dropped open. *Brian?* "He's a criminal? But-"

"Yes, last arrested ten years ago."

"Ten years ago? He still looks like that now. I even thought him too young to be studying for a masters degree. And what's with that surname, Alchez, on his arrest plate?"

"The name he gave you, Brian Chalmers, is one of his alternate identities."

"I don't believe it."

"He's never been enrolled in a University degree, short or long. Heck, he didn't even finish high school. He dropped out at sixteen," Schultz informed her.

Emily couldn't believe what she was hearing. The man who'd gone out of his way to protect her earlier was a criminal.

"But... He said he's studying cybersecurity. He seemed to know a bit about computers. More than your average Joe."

"That's because he's a hacker."

"A hacker?"

"Freelance," the other detective stepped in. "Hacker for hire, for anyone willing to pay his seemingly outrageous fee. His clients have ranged from large corporations wanting to get leverage against staff all the way through to the black market, assisting gangs and dealers to clean their funds."

Emily's blood boiled as her frustrations built. She didn't want to listen to them accusing her savior. Incensed, she paced back and forth under the pergola, hands on her hips.

"I don't understand. Why did he save me?"

"Did he?" the detective asked.

"Yeah." Emily snapped around to face the detective. She stared at him. "When that lunatic gunman let loose outside my apartment, he got me out of there."

"Okay, then." The detective nervously shifted his feet. "How did the gunman keep finding you?"

"We were constantly on the run. The men were always hot on our heels." Emily paused for a moment before something clicked in her mind. She looked at Schultz. "I'd think we'd lost them but then... Out of the blue, they would appear, hot on our heels."

Schultz looked up at the detective, who, without any change of expression, nodded. It appeared they were talking telepathically – even though Emily knew that wasn't possible.

"We've been investigating Brian for the last five years." Schultz turned to Emily, his face solemn. "Soon after his release from a shortened prison term, he resumed his services. He was quiet for the first few months, doing low-key corporate projects. Then he went dark, about six years ago. Since then we've arrested him many times but the charges never stuck. Some politician would always step in, and then the charges were dropped, no explanation, just disappeared. He would be a free man again."

"Then how on earth did you manage to arrest him ten years ago?" Emily demanded.

"He was sloppy," the other detective said. "He was young and naïve. At that time, he hadn't learnt to hide his digital trail yet."

"What doesn't make sense," Emily said, "is what he was doing in my apartment building. It's a carded system. You can't get into the elevators without your card."

"We don't have an answer yet. We didn't even know, till just now, that Brian was in the city. He's usually lurking in one of the suburbs near the city's airports."

"Why aren't they using him to hack my bank accounts, my emails?"

"They've probably already done that."

"You might be right," Emily mused. "My TV was playing up when the breaking news headline was televised. The one for that hostage situation at the Bank of Victoria. I didn't think much of it at the time. Just chalking it off to dodgy digital reception."

"We need to get some uniforms," Schultz said looking up at the other detective. "Get them to secure the apartment. I need that apartment searched in its entirety. Bag anything that doesn't belong in there, especially anything that looks like it could've been used to survey the apartment." The detective stepped away to make the necessary phone calls.

Schultz returned his attention to Emily. His face had softened, no longer rigid and stern.

"We've received intel..." His voice lowered. "Brian's been working solely with a Chinese syndicate for the last six months."

"O-kay."

"In the last few days, our computer techs-"

"Legalized hackers."

"Computer techs." Schultz smiled but his smile disappeared as quickly as it had appeared. He continued, "They've made some startling discoveries."

"As one may expect — it's their job."

"How long have you been investigating your current case?"

"My current case? I'm about to start one. That's why I'm back in town."

"No. The one all over your kitchen table and wall."

"Oh, that one. A little while. Just in my off time."

"Our computer techs have been making similar connections."

"Okay. But lately I haven't made much headway. I still haven't worked out how they're all connected."

"The missing connection," the other detective said, returning to their conversation, "is that it's led us to believe the lead investor in the Chinese-led international syndicate is in bed with the head honcho at Bank of Victoria."

"Andrew? Cook?"

"That's him. Brian has been working his magic with this syndicate."

"That... That's why he seemed to know a lot about Andrew, most of which hasn't been in the headlines." Emily couldn't believe what she'd just heard. It was starting to make sense. "Do you think...? No, it can't be." Emily shook her head.

"That Brian is in bed with the men who were after you two today?"

"Yeah, but that's ludicrous."

Emily was still in denial. She still couldn't properly comprehend it all and was finding it hard to believe that someone would double-cross, deliberately put someone's life in danger as well as their own.

"Maybe not. We're only going where the leads send us."

"So, what if I jump on the next plane outta here and lay low for a while?" Emily asked.

"This syndicate... They're dark. Hands in many pockets across the globe. It'd be hard to find a place that hasn't been infiltrated by this gang."

"I'm sure I could find somewhere."

"Have they made any demands? Requested anything?"

Emily thought about it. The only thing she'd received was a set of co-ordinates. "Nothing. Only this set of co-ordinates."

Emily pulled out her phone and brought up on the screen what Brian had sent her. Schultz read it before handing it to his other colleague.

"He was sending you into Chinatown?" the detective asked.

"Yeah. I was near there earlier, but the pursuers were right behind me. Brian told me I'd be looked after. I'd be given protection and anything else I'd need."

"Protection? You need to stay away from there."

"Why?"

Emily's question went unanswered. The detective pointed his finger at her, indicating to be quiet, while he made a phone call, speaking in what she believed was Mandarin.

Even though her Chinese was rough, she tried to make out his end of the conversation. He wasn't giving much away, just kept looking down at her phone and quite likely passing on details she'd just relayed to them moments before.

There was silence, then her phone was handed back to her. She stared at the screen until the screen turned itself off.

Something didn't feel right. The city felt like it was closing in around her.

Looking up, she asked Schultz, "Are we finished?" Her hand closed around her cell phone at the same time.

Chapter 22

Squealing tires made Emily jump. She turned around to face the direction of the disturbance while instinctively inching back to the farthest part of the pergola.

A car was drifting from Bourke Street into Spring Street. Two more cars followed, drifting as well as they navigated the corner and accelerating as they straightened.

Schultz and his colleague jumped into action, guns pointing at the oncoming cars.

More of their colleagues appeared out of nowhere — two more plain-clothes and a dozen uniforms. A uniformed officer was calling the incident in as he approached the assembling officers.

Schultz and his colleagues were soon gathered along the

one-way entrance into Spring Street. Emily turned towards Nicholson Street. No one was positioned there.

The cars were now half a block away and approaching fast.

Emily looked around. A few women screamed and ran away from the hotspot but most people were absorbed in their own lives, headphones and cell phones to notice what was going on around them.

Unable to find any more undercovers, she stepped out from under the pergola and sought protection on the other side of the concrete wall, beneath the young weeping willows.

Crouched low, Emily listened as the cars neared.

Peeking carefully over the wall, she saw the front car had its rear passenger window wound down. What looked like a barrel was sticking out of the car. She caught a glimpse of the passenger — who was sporting a similar scar as the gunman who'd chased her earlier.

Can't be!

She dropped out of sight behind the wall just as gun fire erupted. Around her people screamed and began running around like ants in a disrupted ants' nest.

Crouching, she scurried along the concrete wall to the other end. She stopped about a meter from the end, right before the solid wall gave way to narrow columns of concrete, like cell bars.

The gunfire stopped and the first car began to burn rubber.

Through the gaps in the wall, Emily caught another glimpse of the passenger as the car passed her. It sped away, not even slowing down for the red traffic light, cutting straight through the intersection.

How did they find me here?

About ten seconds of silence later, a second set of gunfire erupted.

Second car, Emily thought.

She watched the detectives as they continued to fire back. Their firearms were no match against the shooters. Some detectives fell, clutching their wounds. One fell where Emily had been standing only moments before.

A third set of gunfire started before the second car had passed her. This one wasn't burning rubber; they were just getting out of there.

In the distance, Emily heard sirens. They were still a long way away.

Rapid gunfire replaced the screams. Car brakes squealed as they suddenly needed to swerve around pedestrians running every which way.

The unwounded detectives and nearby passersby began attending to the fallen. Some had phones in their hands, probably talking to the emergency services or their loved ones.

Emily looked after the cars that had sped off. Other than the wounded, there wasn't any evidence they'd been there.

She scanned the scene. Her eyes settled on what she was certain was Schultz's back, his curly locks resting on his collar. Relieved he didn't appear injured, she slipped from the garden and onto the busy Nicholson Street.

In front of her were at least four lanes of traffic, with a two-lane tram line segregating the two directions of traffic flow.

To her left was a tram stop and an empty line, the other direction empty as well.

On the other side of the street, a high wrought-iron fence bordered off a lush lawn area. Scanning the fence line towards the tram stop and a busy intersection, she noticed an opening half way along.

Down the right side of the fence she saw another opening, and through it a path running parallel to the tall vegetation. But it was within the detectives' line of sight, and there was no cover between her position and the park.

No, it was too risky. They'd be looking for her in a matter of minutes, and the cavalry would follow a few minutes behind them. She needed to get away. Now.

She surveyed the park area again. It was also very open, but it was a direct route to the adjoining street.

Behind her, everyone was still busy. Emily walked across the street at a normal pace so as not to attract unwanted attention.

She let out a small sigh of relief when she made it across unnoticed but didn't stop. She walked directly to the park entrance. A tram pulled up at the nearby tram stop as she walked through the gates.

Perfect timing, Emily thought. She couldn't see the oriental garden or the detectives.

The enormity of the open space hit Emily as she began to walk across the park, keeping to the center of the footpath. It was open, with a few trees near the fence line and the rest set to grass.

Looking around, she spotted a group of Asian tourists approaching from behind, who were taking photos of everything and hadn't noticed her walking slowly.

Slowing her walking pace more, she pulled out her cell phone and stared at her black screen while watching them out of the corner of her eye.

The group took up the entire width of the footpath and pushed Emily around as they passed her. Biting her lip, she kept her head down.

As the last of the group passed, she walked in sync with them, moving from the center of the path to the left side of the group, the opposite side to Nicholson Street.

Gradually making her way up the side of the group, she pulled a loose set of headphones from one of the tourists' bags and continued walking a little faster, until she was just in front of them, just enough to look like she was still part of their group.

So far so good.

They were so wrapped up in each other's chatter and the photos on their devices they hadn't even noticed her.

Emily lost her cover when the group stopped at a water feature positioned about half way along the footpath. She contemplated staying with them, using their cover, but she couldn't afford to stay in one area for too long.

Picking up her pace, she made a beeline for the park's exit.

Stepping onto the street, Emily scanned the road and parked cars. The parked cars were empty, by what she could see, and the people traveling in their vehicles were minding their own business. Not one of them gave Emily any attention.

Eyeing a van parked alongside the park, she took refuge behind it. Not the best protection, but it was enough to keep hidden from Schultz for a minute.

Up the street she saw more wrought-iron fencing and open space. Too open. It would be too risky.

Across the street was a tall office building with a turnstile at the front door. She could hide in there, but it would only be a matter of time before she'd be escorted out by security. No, she couldn't afford to draw any attention. You just never knew when people suddenly acquired a crystal-clear memory when questioned by the police.

No, she needed to stay away from people. She couldn't risk anyone seeing her. She didn't want her whereabouts monitored, by anyone.

The next few buildings all had their doors shut. Looking farther down the street, she saw a café and a few more buildings, all with heavy wooden doors, and all shut.

Still with no idea where to take refuge, Emily crossed the street. She'd just gotten to the other side when something caught her attention in the distance.

It wouldn't be the worst idea I've ever had, Emily thought.

She paused, protected from view by another parked vehicle, looking at the spire dominating the skyline.

It's not too far away, Emily thought, *and today of all days it should be quiet, if not desolate.*

She considered the street ahead. A lane causing a break in the row of parked vehicles left her vulnerable.

The sirens were growing louder. Turning around, Emily watched a police car speed through the intersection towards the shooting scene.

Pulling her jacket off, she tied it around her waist and hooked up the headphones to her phone. She didn't activate any music, although she could go with some R&B right about now. She needed to be alert. On the lookout for everything and everyone around her. The last thing she needed was for someone to jump her because she was enjoying some tunes.

After ensuring the area was safe, she began a light jog up the footpath towards the spire, avoiding all eye contact and pretending to be focused on her stride and breathing — which turned out to be more necessary than first imagined. She hadn't done so much training, let alone running, since she'd been training at her highest peak.

She remembered her father telling her she had to learn self-defense if she was to go freelance with her career. He hadn't cared too much about what type it was; she just had to be able to protect herself.

While she was fresh in the workforce, Emily had flirted with all different forms until she'd settled on Muay Thai. That was ten years ago, a time when she enjoyed the vigorous training, the feeling of being alive and fit.

Emily reached the grounds of the cathedral without anyone shooting at her.

"It can't be this easy. Can it?"

Chapter 23

The cathedral towered over Emily as she stepped up the front steps, a shadow cast over the entrance.

Reaching the top of the stairs, she paused, unable to take another step closer.

A shiver skittered up her back.

No, I can't do it. Not to these innocent people, she thought as she stared at the small congregation inside.

Sitting down on the stairs, she pulled up a map of Melbourne on her cell phone. A flashing arrow indicated the location in Chinatown Brian, or whatever his name was, had sent her to. Her meeting point was now across the city. The direct route indicated a good twenty minutes' walk, and that was if the traffic allowed.

Looking at the proposed route, Emily decided it wasn't going to work. It was taking her directly past the place where she'd left Schultz. It would now be swarming with police. Roads would be blocked, sidewalks cordoned off. No, that way had too much heat.

Emily sought out a new option. She was torn between Brian's plan, and his reassurance that she'd get protection, and Schultz's warning that Brian was connected to the syndicate.

She dragged the map around, zooming in. Thick red lines showed up — heavy traffic, possibly congested. She zoomed in further.

"Son of a-"

She bit her tongue.

The congested streets were all around the banking district of Collins Street.

Zooming out until her current location came into view, she realized it would be less than ten minutes away if she went directly there.

"Don't be silly, Em. What can you do to help that farmer? For all you know, he could have that place rigged," she said to herself.

She received a few concerned looks from tourists taking pictures of the cathedral, who slowly stepped away from her.

Looking around the top end of the city square, Emily saw an alternate route. It was taking her to the right of the city square, through a dense park on its outskirts. Then she could enter the building through the rear. It was a longer route, but there should be less people and fewer chances for interaction with the public or for being noticed.

She turned her screen off.

Focus! I need to find shelter somewhere and work out who on earth is chasing me and why, Emily told herself. The reason why Schultz had been questioning her for so long earlier, in the open, was still a mystery to her.

Unless... Emily shook her head. No, it couldn't be. She couldn't imagine Schultz allowing anyone he worked with, someone he trusted to have his back, to cross the line. But it was the only way the gunmen would have been able to locate them quickly.

A distant ping snapped her out of her daze. Must be a notification on her phone. Thinking it was just another game alert, she ignored it. The phone pinged again. Sighing, Emily unlocked her screen.

It was a private message from one of her social media platforms. She didn't recognize the avatar, and there was no descriptive text indicating the start of the message.

Another message came through as she was still looking at the screen. This time it included the following text: Li Global Investments. SOS. ILLEGALLY acquired by BOV.

That piqued her interest but she was still skeptical. Clicking on the message, she waited for the app to load, certain it would just be another person leading her up the garden path. Again.

She read the remaining message.

> *Sorry for this message arriving out of the blue. I need your help.*

I'm a seventh-generation farmer of our family property. Our land was taken from my family. We were forcibly removed and threatened with criminal charges if we re-entered.

I found your contact details while scouring through the bank's email correspondence. You were copied in the correspondence relating to my family farm.

I'm running out of options.

I need your help. Now.

Regards, Harry Fry

The cursor blinked at her, waiting for her to type a reply.

"Harry Fry," she said to herself, looking up from her phone. Could he be the real Harry Fry? Or an impostor? Someone with too much time on their hands and a bad sense of humor.

She clicked on his profile picture and his profile details loaded. There wasn't much on there, just the bare minimum required to open an account.

She closed the applications. Probably another scammer taking advantage of the situation unfolding in downtown Melbourne. But if she did manage to make it to the banking district in one piece, she could probably verify it.

Peering over her shoulder into the cathedral, Emily wondered what she should do. The flicker of the candles calmed her.

Her phone pinged again. She ignored it. She had her own problems to worry about.

Her phone rang. She jumped.

A video call was coming through from the same social media application as the earlier message, and the same user.

"What the hell!" Emily said as she accepted the call.

The video stream came through speckled, as if a storm was interfering with the broadcast. It was streaming from inside an office. Some type of abstract artwork adorned the white wall. To the side, Emily could distinguish a window and the tops of skyscrapers beyond it.

The call was being made from a great distance. It looked plausible. *For now,* Emily thought.

"Thirty seconds. Get to the point," Emily said into her phone.

A tired, middle-aged, tanned, Caucasian man appeared on the screen. Emily was surprised but kept her composure.

"Counting."

"You look like you've been through the wars," the man replied.

"Twenty seconds."

"I'm at the Bank of Victoria headquarters. I came here to speak to the boss. The one who undersigned the theft."

"How do I know you are where you say you are?"

The screen moved around to an anxious younger lady. Emily recognized her straight away as Andrew's secretary from her research notes and by the faint outline of her name on her name tag. Then the caller returned to the screen.

"You know who that is?" he asked.

"Yes. Yes, I do. And you are?"

"Can you help me or not?"

"I'm not sure what you expect I can do. I'm just a pen pusher, a secretary," Emily lied.

"You're going to get my family farm back. By the close of business today."

Glancing at the time on her fitness watch, Emily felt like laughing but contained herself. She wasn't a miracle worker, but she also didn't know what frame of mind Harry was in. She didn't want to have the deaths of the secretary or other bank staff on her conscience.

"That gives you," he continued, "five hours."

"Five hours?" Emily repeated.

"I didn't stutter."

"Look, you seem like a hard-working, straight-talking kinda guy. Wouldn't it be easier to talk to Andrew? Get him to resolve this?"

"Would if he were here. He did a disappearing act when I stormed the offices. Lookin' at his emails and paperwork, it's all a scam."

"What makes you think it's a scam?" Emily quizzed.

"I'll have this fine lady here forward you a video. A video of the day they tore my family apart."

"Why can't you tell me?"

"You have five hours to get my farm back."

Emily was left staring at her phone's home screen. The call disconnected.

"This guy has got to be kidding."

A fleeting moment passed while Emily entertained the idea of this being a big set-up by the people chasing her. A trap.

Her phone vibrated and a message notification came through.

"Sharon Hann, video," Emily read.

A shortened hyperlink was attached.

Skeptical, she hesitated, her fingers hovering over the hyperlink. Another message from Sharon came through.

Emily read the new message. "Click on the link. Please. He has a gun pointed at me. It's not a corrupt link. It's genuine. Sharon Xo" Emily shook her head at a cat-face emoji that followed Sharon's signature.

Chapter 24

"Here goes." Emily pressed the link and another application opened. She hit 'play' and a small circle appeared with a strobe of light circling around it. A moment later, after her phone had buffered enough of the file, the video started.

The recording was horrible, and the footage was all over the place. Emily felt dizzy and struggled to focus on what was happening.

By the angle and the way the camera was moving, it appeared the cameraman had been wearing something like one of those cameras you could strap onto your forehead.

The cameraman paused for a moment and moved the camera around. To one side, a modest machinery shed was positioned on a small rise. Not too big — just enough to fit a medium-sized tractor, a Ute and a hay baler. Behind and to the side, fertile paddocks were on full display, with cattle happily grazing in the lush green fields.

A little farther around was a small shed with a small cemented entranceway, some railings on the inside and a small door to the side — possibly a dairy.

The camera moved around some more until it focused on a modest brick home with manicured green lawns and blooming garden. A freshly painted wire fence bordered the house.

Emily thought there was nothing lavish about the farm. To her, this wasn't a big purchase, and nothing stuck out that would've caused him to miss some repayments or default on his mortgage. So far, the property looked like it was maintained by a hard-working farmer who was having a fair crack at trying to make a nice home for himself and his family.

"Harry Fry," a male voice spoke over the video footage. He sounded close. She assumed it was the cameraman talking.

"Dairy farmer from Gippsland, Victoria, Australia. Ten past nine in the morning. 1,305-acre property being foreclosed-"

Footage of the papers appeared as the cameraman's head lowered.

"No. He's not, is he?" Emily said. "How unprofessional."

The camera focused on the writing on the front page. The Bank of Victoria logo was clearly visible in the top right corner, along with a memo-style document on the front highlighting the bare minimum details of that day's events, including Harry's name and address at the top.

She couldn't believe what she was seeing. The cameraman flicked through the sheets of paper, right there in front of the camera. If she had paused on each page, she would've been able to read everything to do with the case.

"Foreclosure due to no longer conducting a viable operation."

The cameraman turned. Emily almost dropped her phone.

"Son of a-" Her mouth dropped open.

The man at the center of her investigation was standing next to the cameraman. Andrew Cook.

"Is this correct?" the cameraman asked.

"Of course it is." Andrew waved it off. "Come on, let's get this over and done with." He looked at his watch. "I have places to be today, and it's one helluva drive back to the city."

The cameraman turned around farther to his right. Four men stood with their arms crossed, only their eyes visible through their balaclavas, fixed on the cameraman.

Emily was getting an awful feeling in her stomach again. Something didn't seem right about any of this.

The video continued to play. The cameraman knocked at the front door.

There was no answer.

He tried again. Nothing.

The cameraman turned around, his back to the door.

Andrew was giving hand signals to two of the masked men. One pulled a gun out of his back pocket, and the other batons. They quickly moved around to the side of the house, neither of them making a sound as they walked over the gravel.

The cameraman stood aside while Andrew knocked on the front door.

Screams echoed through the recording.

The video footage continued to roll.

A women's scream was heard in the background again.

Andrew indicated for one of the men to remain while the other walked in front of him. The cameraman followed Andrew around to the rear of the house.

Emily shook her head, her mouth and eyes wide open. She couldn't believe what she was watching.

Two children were being held in the arms of one of the men while the other held the woman around her waist. The woman was yelling out, tears streaming down her face as she tried to reach for her children.

"You have no right to be here," she hissed at Andrew.

"You're now trespassing on the property of Bank of Victoria. If you do not leave immediately, you will be arrested."

"On what grounds?" She spat at his feet.

If it wasn't for the severity of what was happening, Emily would've normally cheered the woman.

"You want me to shut her up?" the man holding the woman asked, pressing a gun against the back of her head.

Andrew shook his head and the masked man tucked the gun away. At that moment, Harry's wife quickly stretched her hand above her head and grabbed the man's balaclava, pulling it off before he pinned both arms behind her back.

"Oi," a deep male's voice yelled.

The camera panned around to a farmer running across the yard towards them, dressed in worn jeans, dirt-stained flannelette shirt, and a tired outback hat.

Andrew crossed his arms and positioned himself between the farmer and the woman and children. He tried to blow away a few blow flies who dared to fly near him to not success; they continued to fly around his face, some landing on his back.

The farmer slowed as he approached the group.

"Victoria, are you and the kids alright?" Harry asked as he looked towards his family, his woman nodding, then to Andrew. "What's going on? Why have you got my wife and kids restrained?"

"Harry Fry?" Andrew asked.

"Yeah. Who the hell are you?"

Andrew grabbed the papers from the cameraman and flung them into Harry's chest.

"You are now trespassing on the property of the Bank of Victoria."

"Bank of Victoria? Who on earth are they?"

"The bank who now manage this property."

"This is wrong." Harry flicked through the first couple of pages. "This isn't the bank who holds an interest in this property."

"According to this paperwork, yes, we do. You need to remove yourself and your family from this property immediately."

"This is bullshit. Answer me this. Where is the

correspondence from this so-called bank advising us we're losing the property?"

Harry waved the papers.

"I'm under instruction." The cameraman stepped towards Harry. "This property is to be vacated immediately."

"I don't care. I'm calling my lawyer," Harry said. He pointed to his family. "Don't leave this yard. Right."

Harry tapped away at his phone.

Andrew yelled out. Emily couldn't understand the language he was speaking; it was neither English nor Mandarin, her second language.

The video showed a man running around the corner of the house and Andrew pointing his head towards Harry. The masked man ran to Harry as he was about to hit dial on his phone. Taking Harry by surprise, the man grabbed him by his arms and pinned them to his back.

Harry wiggled. The masked man who'd led Andrew and the cameraman around the back grabbed onto one of his pinned arms.

Andrew waved them off.

The men dragged the family away. Frantic screams and struggles fell on deaf ears.

"This is downright illegal," Harry yelled over his shoulder. "You've messed with the wrong family this time."

Emily couldn't believe what she was watching.

One of the men holding Harry struck him on the rear of his head. His head bowed down, his body going limp. He was finally quiet. A bloodcurdling scream erupted from his wife.

The camera focused on Andrew, who was brushing his suit down and swiping flies away.

"That was easier than I thought." A deep belly laugh burst from Andrew. "Now for you. Your job here is done. Forward the edited video footage to my office first thing in the morning."

The cameraman didn't reply. Instead, he quietly walked off, video still recording. He turned to catch Andrew making a phone call.

"It is in our possession," he was saying. "We'll start the process of having the property signed over to you."

The video stopped and Emily closed the app.

"Shit. What on earth is going on?" Emily asked herself. "None of this makes sense."

She opened her messaging app and located Harry's last message. She hesitated. Her fingers hovered above the call button.

I can't help everyone, Emily thought.

She was usually the one to say yes to everyone and everything. But not today. She couldn't. There was no way she'd have time to help Harry and keep herself alive.

She loaded the video again, this time paying careful attention to Andrew. She fast forwarded through the bits where he wasn't in the footage, then paused the video and re-wound it a little bit. Played it at half speed.

Emily paused the footage. The moment after the wife pulled the man's balaclava off. She'd frozen the footage shortly after the unmasked man had walked past the camera.

"I don't believe it."

She looked up and recalled the incidences from earlier that day, the ones where he'd featured, focusing on his facial features.

"It can't be." Emily returned to the frozen image on her phone. From the corner of the screen, his icy eyes were piercing her, right over the burn scar that ran down the side of his face.

She dialed Harry.

It rang twice. She was about to hang it up at the third ring when the line connected. Emily heard heavy breathing on the other side.

"I don't know what on earth is going on here," she said, "but I'm in. We need to take a stand. Together."

She was already regretting her acceptance. Schultz's response was already running through her mind, advising her to leave it to the police. But she'd seen enough. The banks taking advantage of the smaller guys. Goons chasing her half way across Melbourne, shooting to kill.

"I thought you would be. What made you change your mind?"

"I believe the same people who are after you are also after me. What exactly do you need me to do?"

"I... er... I have a lot of information here. Can you get here?"

"No. No, I don't think so. The police have the surrounding blocks barricaded. By now, there'll probably be snipers focused on all areas of your building."

"Damn. Okay." Harry paused.

Emily heard Sharon in the background.

"We can upload the information to a cloud. But we need to act fast. It'll only be a matter of time before the servers are blocked."

"Good thinking, Sharon," Emily called out.

"Hang tight. Keep alive. I'll have Sharon send something through as soon as we get it up. And if you can, I need you to get this information to your contacts. Expose what's going on here."

"Very well," Emily replied.

The call disconnected.

"Hope they know whom they're up against," Emily said as she tucked her phone away.

The wind had picked up. Unusual, as there hadn't been much wind all day. But this was Melbourne — four seasons in one day was the usual order of the day.

Coming from the side of the cathedral, she could hear a motor running. A chopper?

From where she was sitting, Emily couldn't see anything. Whatever it was sounded like it was hovering. Low. It couldn't be the police — Schultz would've made contact with her first.

She heard something land on the ground. A second later she heard someone zipping down a line.

Emily looked to her side. A small hedge stood in front of a wrought-iron fence. It'd been a while since she'd jumped fences. She shuddered at the thought of getting caught on the metal points.

In front of her, the gates she'd entered through. It was exposed. Open ground. Too risky.

She shook her head, not believing what she was thinking. Running around the side of the cathedral, she headed towards the wrought-iron fence. Half way along the fence she noticed a red metal box, about half her height.

She ran towards it.

Digging deep and in one swift movement, she launched herself onto the box then propelled herself over the fence, grabbing the spokes and pushing herself over.

Emily landed in a crouched position facing the street. Looking up, she noticed blades from a helicopter hovering on the other side of the cathedral.

To her left a tram bell dinged. She looked around. The tram stop wasn't too far away, about half a block. She sprinted towards it, dodging traffic and being careful to not scare any of the drivers and set off another chain of unfortunate events.

For once, luck was on her side. She got to the tram stop as the tram arrived.

Stepping onto the tram, she swiped her watch on the ticketing system screen. Everyone either had their headphones stuck in their ears or their eyes were glued to their cell phones.

The tram was about three small carriages long and half full. It began moving as she took an aisle seat about half way down the middle carriage. Looking back at the cathedral, she saw fully black-clothed armed men mill around it. A few remained at the front of the cathedral, their guns pointed into the building and at the main entrance. The remaining men moved around to the side of the building, their guns sweeping around, surveying the area.

Emily was left with a niggling thought as the tram rattled along the tramline. *How did they know I was here?*

Chapter 25

Back in the comfort of the concrete jungle, her tram slowed as it arrived at the next stop. Standing at the door, Emily noticed a dirty work van pull into a car park opposite the tram stop. The driver of the van caught her eye but quickly glanced down at something in his van.

Emily shrugged it off. The van was parked at the front of a bank. He was probably there for business.

The tram doors opened and Emily was the only one to step off. She felt vulnerable standing in the middle of the road. Taking a deep breath, she crossed the road and made her way back up the street, towards a building where she hoped the contents inside her deposit box would make her day a lot easier and give her some much-needed backup.

Approaching the building located at number one hundred, she glanced over her shoulder. The van was gone.

Get a grip. Not everyone in the city is after you today, Emily thought.

She stepped through the reinforced glass door, which closed as soon as she was inside.

"Welcome, ma'am," a very well-dressed gentleman greeted her and bowed slightly. "How can we be of service today?"

Emily nodded her approval; no name tag. Tidy, and going by the sharp edges of his suit, it was probably freshly steam-cleaned. Clean-shaven, face and head. No noticeable tattoos.

Emily held back a chuckle as she felt around in her bag, imagining him hiding a sinister tattoo somewhere on him.

Focused, she finally fumbled across its smooth surface. With it between her two fingers, she pulled it out and presented it to the man.

"Very well."

He inspected the token.

On one side, the token had a border around its circumference. It looked like an ancient alphabet but Emily wasn't too sure; maybe it was just a jumble of shapes. Inside the decorative border, an image took up most of the negative space. A triquetra, or as Emily loved to call it, a Celtic knot. She found it much easier to say and remember.

No one had really explained it to her, nor had she sought out answers. The token simply lived in a dark corner, in the bottom of her bag. All she knew was that the establishments displaying the same symbol as her token were able to help her.

The gentleman pulled out a pocket magnifying glass and placed it right up against the token. He studied the image.

"Happy with what you see?" Emily asked, trying to look over his shoulder.

He put the magnifying piece back in his pocket and handed the token back to Emily.

"This way, ma'am."

Emily followed the man to a glass sliding door. He paused.

"What's wrong?" Emily asked.

The man pointed to a device.

"Your personal identification code and your hand, ma'am."

Emily's heart skipped a beat. She didn't remember seeing this biometric hand reader when she'd last visited, here or in any of the other establishments.

She punched in the only code she'd used before then lifted her hand up to the device, hovering.

"Is there a problem, ma'am?"

"No. Not at all. These things, technology, it kind of freaks me out."

"It won't take long. Your hand needs to be there just long enough for the scanner register to check that you are who you say you are."

Holding her breath, Emily placed her hand down on the reader. Closing her eyes, she held her breath, expecting alarms to be set off at any second.

There was nothing. She pried one eye open.

A door unlocked with a dull click.

"Very well, Destiny Phillips. This way, ma'am." The man

walked through the partially opened door.

Emily couldn't believe it. She stared between the device and her hand. Illuminated on the screen was an alias name. One she was advised would be used for these situations.

"We don't have much time to reach the next security point," the man said with some urgency in his tone. He was now half way down a long corridor and his pace was quickening.

Emily pulled herself together and quickly caught up with him, her steps thundering down the corridor.

By the time she reached him, he had his face near a wall, and a blue light was scanning his eyes. A moment later a second door, a heavy metal one, opened by hydraulics.

"Down the stairs, ma'am. We're almost there."

Emily felt a little stuffy. She waved her hand in front of her face but it didn't help.

Putting one foot in front of the other, she descended the stairs. One step at time. But as she neared the half way point, she was taking them two or three at a time.

She pulled at her shirt's neckline. It felt as though it was closing in on her throat. Her fingers felt warm and clammy. Fumbling on the last couple of steps, she almost misplaced her footing as she placed her foot on the floor.

"You all right, ma'am?" The man stepped in, supporting her arm as she regained her balance.

"Yeah." Emily straightened herself and smiled at him. "I'll be all right, just need to watch my footing next time."

"This way."

He directed Emily to the middle of three vaults. Each one was about twice her height.

Another man, no name tag or any form of identification on him either but dressed in a similar suit, nodded at the man who had accompanied her down here.

He twisted and turned a few handles and the vault opened. Slowly, he pushed the vault door wide open.

"After you, ma'am." He directed Emily inside.

Stepping in, Emily couldn't believe her eyes. This room was big enough to fit her whole apartment inside it, at least three, maybe even four times.

Columns of silver-edged cabinets lined the interior space, floor to ceiling. The man walked past her and proceeded up the far-left corridor. He stopped about half way down.

"Your key, ma'am?"

He held a key in his hand, which was attached to a steel line pulley coming from under his suit jacket.

Emily pulled her purse out of her bag and rummaged through it. Receipts fell into her bag. She found the key tucked away in a zipped pocket, almost making its way through a small tear in the stitching.

She pulled it out and presented it.

He looked down at her key, then to Emily, before glancing back to the key.

"Very well." He directed her into the second to last station.

Emily turned the token over. The inscription on the reverse side read 253.

She read the numbers on the sea of deposit boxes. Her eyes

skimmed over the upper small ones. They didn't interest her. She was after the bigger ones down the bottom.

"256, 255," Emily read each one.

She paused in front of box 253. She checked the inscription on her token against the deposit box. It was a match.

"This one." Emily turned to face the man and pointed at box 253.

The man placed his key in and turned the lock. He stepped aside and indicated for Emily to do the same. She carefully placed the key in the lock and turned the key. The locking mechanism clicked and the door opened.

Emily pulled out the inner container and closed the door. It was a little heavier than she remembered.

The man first removed his key and then Emily removed hers.

"This way, ma'am. With your box."

He directed her away from the lockers and towards a corner near the front of the vault. She held the box against her stomach, leaning back a little and allowing her body to take most of the weight off her arms.

He pulled a curtain aside and directed her in. The small cubicle she was in had an appearance more sterile than hospital walls. White-washed walls, black tiles and a single fluorescent light humming above. It even had the pungent hospital smell.

They appeared to have cut costs in this room. Nothing screamed richness in here, she thought as she continued to look around.

In the center of the room, a plain white wooden table sat

with a simple green velvet mat in its center. Beneath the table, about half way down, a tray was secured to the table legs. On it was a wad of red velvet bags with the company's logo embroidered on its front.

I won't be needing those hideous bags, Emily thought. *They scream 'mug me!'*

"I'll be just outside if you need anything, ma'am."

"Thank you." Emily nodded. The curtain closed.

When the curtain stopped moving, Emily placed her hands on the corners of the table and stared down at the box that now lay on top of the green velvet mat.

Chapter 26

Unlocking the safety deposit box, Emily carefully pulled the lid back. A smile appeared on her face at the sight of the contents.

She pulled out first a variety of passports, flicking through them, all under different aliases and nationalities.

"Impressive," she whispered and placed them to the side.

Next, she pulled out wads of cash. She estimated about ten thousand dollars in each bundle, denominations from across the globe. Enough to get her out of trouble.

The box now appeared empty. She fumbled with its base until it gave way. Pulling back the light piece of wood that camouflaged the bottom half, she smiled. Inside was a red shaggy bag. She pulled it out and placed it on the table alongside the deposit box.

Carefully, she placed the fake bottom back in and pushed the deposit box to the side. The noise made by the metal base scraping along the wooden table pierced her ears.

She shuddered.

"All good, ma'am?" a male voice on the other side of the curtain asked. The curtains moved near the edge of the curtain rail.

"Yeah, all good. Sorry about that."

There was silence. The curtain stopped moving.

Opening the red velvet bag, she pulled out each piece until they were all roughly laid out in their correct position on the velvet mat.

Emily inspected each of them individually and then proceeded to count the contents of a small box.

Happy with their condition, she placed everything inside the red bag.

She sifted through the passports. One for England, United States, Romania, Canada, Morocco, Brazil, Russia and New Zealand.

When she saw the New Zealand one, she put it straight back in the compartment box; too close to home.

Beneath the New Zealand passport, there was one Emily didn't recognize.

"Kingdom of Saudi Arabia," Emily whispered, opening the passport.

A photo of her was on the inside, her head covered in a black headscarf.

Emily tried to recall if she'd ever worn one. She couldn't think of it. She studied the photo. *Whoever has put this together has done a wonderful job photo-shopping it on.*

"Nadia Bunting," she read the name that appeared alongside her photo. "Seriously?"

She flicked through the pages; none of them was stamped. A piece of paper landed on the table.

Unfolding it, Emily read the contents.

"Exit papers from Saudi Arabia." She checked the date on her watch. "Two weeks ago. Interesting. Might need this if things go south quickly."

Folding the piece of paper up, she placed it back inside the passport and put it aside with the Russian passport.

The remaining passports she carefully placed back in her safety deposit box.

Grabbing a couple of wads of Saudi Riyal dollars, she counted out approximately 30,000 Riyals and approximately 225,000 Russian Rubles. The remaining wads went back in the box.

"Are you alright in there, ma'am?" the guard asked and paused. Emily suspected he was listening. "Anything we can help you with?" His voice appeared closer.

"Ah, no." She locked the compartment box. "Won't be a moment. I'm almost finished. Sorry for taking so long."

She placed the cash and passports inside a hidden compartment sewn into the side of her bag then took one last look around. Everything had been put away.

"Okay, I'm ready," she yelled out.

The curtain slid along the rail. Pulling both bags over her shoulder, she carried the box out.

After securing the box back in its proper place, she nodded at the guard and left the vault. Outside, the man who'd brought her down there proceeded up the stairs.

He didn't look at her twice. He'd probably seen stranger things in there than her shaggy red bag.

They proceeded to the exit in silence. This time there wasn't any urgency to get through the security checkpoints. As they approached each door, they automatically opened.

Emily glanced around. She'd noticed security cameras everywhere. Not what she wanted, but she was sure they were protecting far better secrets than her modest stash.

"Until next time, Miss Phillips." The man held the exit door for her and nodded to Emily.

"Till next time." She returned the nod and stepped out onto the city street.

She breathed it all in. The fumes filled her lungs again, screeching brakes and drivers blaring their horns pierced her ears.

Chapter 27

The sidewalks were empty, and so were the notifications on her cell phone. Tapping her foot, she took her time looking around. The same work van still lingered in the street. This time it was two car spaces back. It was the same van. Unlike other city vehicles, this one was distinguishable by its thick layer of red dirt. A white spray area marked the front windshield where the wiper blades couldn't reach.

What really stood out on the van was the signwriting along the side wall, which read, *Sydney's Leak-Free Plumbing. The best place to take your leaks.*

"Sydney?" Emily said. "Aren't you a long way from home?"

Unable to see any occupants, she started down the road, turning into a tree-lined one-lane street farther down.

Making sure she didn't bump into any pedestrians, she turned and glanced over her shoulder, taking one last look at the van. Its brake lights flashed.

Although the sight of the lush green leaves made her happy, Emily was on edge. Stepping back to the corner, she leant against the building and poked her head around the corner. The van was gone.

Leaning against the wall, she composed herself.

"You're being silly, Emily. Snap out of it," she told herself.

Emily received a few odd looks from passersby. That was until she waved and gave them a cheesy grin. She chuckled to herself as she watched how quickly they snapped their heads back to the footpath.

The tree-lined street she was on was a one-way street. If someone was after her, she looked around, there should be plenty of places to take cover.

With nothing to lose, she walked quickly to the first laneway; it was only half a city block away. Leaning against the building on the corner, she looked down the lane. She noticed it was only a small block and ran into to a busy street.

The Sydney Plumber's van rolled through the intersection.

Emily pulled her head back. Fingers crossed, she hadn't been spotted. She looked around the corner again. The intersection was empty.

Her eyes on the oncoming traffic, she approached the next laneway. A dead end. It was empty besides a few trashcans and a few staff workers taking their smoking breaks.

Up ahead, she heard a vehicle's horn being punched

repeatedly at the traffic, which had come to a complete stop. Thinking nothing of the repeated honks, she proceeded up the street, moving closer to the congestion and the disgruntled driver.

She soon realized the lane she was navigating was very closed in, with few exit points.

The disgruntled driver was now two car lengths away.

Emily froze.

"This is no coincidence," she whispered. "How on earth are they track-"

Emily looked down at her watch.

"Son of a-"

She ripped it off.

"How stupid can I be?"

Her watch was the only item on her with GPS tracking activated; it was used to help track her daily steps prior to her recommencing training.

Next to her, a motorcyclist was getting ready to close his motorbike storage compartment. When his back was to her, Emily slipped the watch in there and stepped into the closest shop.

The smell of freshly baked bagels flooded the shop and her senses. Keeping an eye on the front door, Emily edged back to the farthest corner, which wasn't far enough in this boutique bakery, maybe only about five people deep.

The motorcyclist revved his engine before speeding up the street on his rear tire.

"Next," a pimply faced teenager bellowed from behind the

counter.

Emily saw everyone look at her. She returned her attention to the shop, realizing it was her turn to order.

"Oh." She waved her hands in front of her. "I'm still looking."

"Next," the kid called.

Emily turned back to the front door.

Growing impatient, she moved a couple of steps towards the door. At that moment, the same dirty plumber's van drove past and sped off.

There was no time to eat. As much as her tummy was detesting her, she resisted the urge. In the distance, she heard blaring horns and metal scraping against metal.

Everyone from neighboring shops flooded the street but Emily remained where she was. She knew what had just happened. It was safer to stay put.

The street soon returned to normality as people quickly grew tired of seeing the aftermath of a van careering into a busy intersection in hot pursuit of a hot-headed motorcyclist.

After waiting a minute, she grabbed a cold, flavored spring water from the drinks fridge next to her. On the way out of the shop, she dropped enough change on the counter to cover the cost of the drink.

Walking down the narrow street, she was wary of every person around her, cautious of anyone and everyone. Double-looking over her shoulder. Ensuring she was alone.

Emily took a right down a quaint little lane. Coffee aromas permeated every nook of the lane. Chairs and tables spilled out onto the street, filled with an assortment of people enjoying the many cuisines on offer.

About half way down, she found a quiet lane that was used for empty milk crates and large trashcans. Pulling a milk crate to the corner, away from the trash, she plonked herself on it, grateful to be off her feet for a few minutes.

Sipping on her drink, it dawned on her it'd been a little while since she'd heard from Harry or Sharon. She pulled out her phone and turned data back on. Straight away, her phone beeped and vibrated like crazy as all the notifications came through.

Chapter 28

Emily scanned through the notifications.

A couple of text messages from Schultz that had been sent five minutes earlier had only just come through to her phone. She shrugged, thinking it was odd they hadn't come through until now; they should've come through as normal messages.

"He can wait," she told herself, flicking past.

A little farther down the list were a couple of messages from an unknown number, received thirty minutes ago. These piqued her interest. She was curious, as she wasn't sure how the stranger got her personal cell phone number. After the Sydney incident, she had only given her number to clients and colleagues.

By now, her phone would've already ran its security checks

over everything that'd come in. She clicked on the first message. It read:

Sorry for taking so long to get this to you.
There's a lot of information. Not just Harry's case. It appears Andrew has been busy over the last six months serving to others the same fate Harry received.
Sharon xo

"I don't even know the cat woman and she's sending me virtual kisses & hugs. Unique."

A cat-face emoji followed Sharon's uncanny signature.

The signature confirmed the sender, and Emily felt reassured. The only other information was a shortened web link.

With her finger hovering over the link, Emily looked around. Everyone was busy minding their own conversations, unaware she was there.

The link opened her web browser and re-directed to a cloud server. Waiting for the information to load, Emily took a couple of swigs of her spring water. It hit the spot, leaving her feeling a little cooler and more refreshed.

The page was taking a while to load. Fumbling through her red shaggy bag, Emily blindly assembled the pieces together. She screwed on the silencer and did a quick check, ensuring it had free movement. Happier, she loaded a full round of ammunition into its mag.

She dropped the red shaggy bag to the ground as she placed

the loaded gun in her other bag, checking for onlookers. But everyone was oblivious to what had just happened, Emily was relieved to see.

Emily checked her phone again. The page had finally loaded. It contained a few folders, each one labelled with a person's name and what looked like a company name.

She touched the first name on the list and tapped her feet on the pavement while the hourglass spun on the screen. Above her, small snippets of sky poked through the tall buildings. Maybe it was just her internet provider deciding to slow the internet down. This wouldn't be the first, nor the last time. One moment she had super-fast data, the next second it slowed down to slower than dial-up speed.

A list of files popped up on the screen. Emily scanned through the content — a variety of emails, letters, contracts, and photos, all dating back to twelve months prior.

Emily opened the contract and scrolled to the bottom.

"Six months ago, and that signature."

She scrolled back through the files and pulled up some letters Harry had allegedly sent to Andrew.

"They're clearly not the same signature, and a poor job at faking it, too. Very nineteen-nighties."

In one corner of the signature, there was a small darkened patch, as if a piece of paper with the signature had been placed on the original document then copied. This small piece of evidence could well be damning Andrew. It could be argued his actions had been premeditated.

Investigating the remaining files, she soon realized there

were many more farmers from Gippsland's dairy region who had been hit by this bank. Farms who'd been held in the family for multiple generations.

Emily pulled up a map of the area and placed a virtual thumb tack on each repossessed farm.

"I'll be damned." Emily sat back and clasped her hand over her mouth. Looking around, she noticed some patrons looking at her, but they quickly returned to their own lives.

Before her was a screen full of virtual thumb tacks. In the center there was a bare patch... until Emily placed the last marker.

"Harry's farm is the missing piece."

Emily sat back, realizing what Sharon and Harry had unraveled. No wonder Harry was pissed.

Returning her attention to her phone, she scrolled to the bottom of the folder list.

The folder read: CONFIDENTIAL

"Ha, we'll see just how confidential it is."

Emily opened the folder and more folders appeared. The first two caught her attention. They read:

PRIVATE

PERSONNEL

She opened the PERSONNEL folder and two pdf files appeared.

EXTINCT

ACTIVE

Emily didn't hesitate and clicked on the ACTIVE file. The document began loading. In the top left corner, a face stared at her. Emily gasped.

The rest of the page finally loaded. A simple table with headings and information formulated beside the photo.

Emily began reading:

NAME:	*FERNANDO DOMINIC*
AGE:	*45*
GENDER:	*MALE*
STATUS:	*ACTIVE*
CITIZEN:	*MEXICO*
PLACE OF BIRTH:	*SPAIN*
YEARS SERVICE:	*FIVE (5)*

SERVICE ACCOMPLISHMENTS:

> *Induction − Jewelry burglary followed by a 100% successful kill rate in all jobs received. Also, very accomplished in recovering bad debts.*

RECENT SERVICE: *Ensuring the smooth transition of the final property in North East Victoria to the investors.*

Emily shuddered.

"One hundred percent," she repeated. "So far, I'm the one percent that's marring his perfect record. Damn. Not his day then, is it?"

She scrolled through the remaining records but didn't recognize any of the other faces. She went through them once more, taking a mental note of their facial features, names, and jobs. She lost count of how many there were after the first ten or so, until he found someone else she recognized.

"Brian?"

She read his record.

NAME:	*RONALDO ALCHEZ*
	(Alias Brian Chalmers and W)
AGE:	*35*
GENDER:	*MALE*
STATUS:	*ACTIVE*
CITIZEN:	*AUSTRALIA*
PLACE OF BIRTH:	*SPAIN*
YEARS SERVICE:	*FIFTEEN (15)*

SERVICE ACCOMPLISHMENTS:

Induction – Accessing government records. Setting up a virtual casino and accessing various global government records. Pivotal in the growth of the syndicate

RECENT SERVICE: *Assisting clients with timely transactions.*

"Damn." Emily leant back onto the brick wall. "This is huge."

An alarm sounded on her phone. In bright red, the number fifteen flashed on her screen.

"Shit, too long."

Emily scrambled through her bag and pulled out an external hard drive. Touching a few buttons, she made a backup to her own personal cloud and sent another to her offline hard drive.

Once all backups were complete, she de-activated her cell

phone data and closed all applications running on the phone. After her hard drive was safely back in her bag, she dialed the last number she'd called.

"Lee," a gruff male voice sounded on the other end.

"Schultz. You're not going–"

"Where are you?"

"Don't worry about that. We have bigger fish to fry."

"Continue." His voice was unchanged.

"You're not going to believe what has been sent to me in the last few minutes."

"Look, Lee, I don't have time for your games. Cut to the chase."

"The hostage situation. The targeted shootings at me. They're all linked."

"How?" His tone was now more curious.

"Information forwarded to me shows correspondence linking them all up. Andrew and these men are all working for that International Chinese Syndicate."

"Holy cow. This changes everything."

"I thought you'd be impressed."

"I need you to get that information to me."

"On one condition."

She could hear Schultz's deep belly laugh.

"Seriously. If this helps our cases, we need that information. You're not going to withhold information on me, are you?"

"You're not going to get your hands on this. Not until you agree."

After a moment of silence, Schultz finally said, "Continue," his voice sounding defeated again.

"The guy holding the secretary hostage. He's recently had his farm allegedly stolen from him and handed over to this syndicate on a silver platter. He wants his farm returned to him, and the same for the other farmers who've had theirs stolen."

"That's a tall order that we need to investigate fully first. If it does prove true and correct, fine, but if the documents have already been processed, it's going to get messy."

"You haven't heard him today. When I spoke to him earlier, he was desperate. He's been trying to make himself heard for months but no one listened. And he claims that also includes you, guys."

The line went silent. She could hear a dull tapping coming from the other line, like a pen hitting a desk.

"Schultz?" Emily asked, not sure if he was still there.

"I'm going to regret this," he finally said. "But you owe me big time. You're coming into protective custody."

"No, I'm not. Where are you?"

"At the office."

"I'll be over there shortly."

Emily disconnected the call and opened the last message from Sharon. She typed in the following message:

All systems go. I'll be in touch.

The phone did its thing and the message popped up saying it had been sent.

She checked the time on her phone. Twenty minutes. *Too*

long. I need to get out of here. NOW.

Chapter 29

Emily savored the lingering coffee aromas one last time before ditching the shaggy red bag, now empty, behind a trashcan and stepping out onto the bustling Collins Street.

Out in the open she didn't feel comfortable. It was too exposed. Wide streets with traffic and trams traveling in both directions were a bad idea.

Down towards her apartment building, the police still had the road cordoned off, and officers were manning the area.

Right next to her building, outside the Subway store, she noticed a man leaning against a tree reading a newspaper. On the opposite side of the road a few people dressed in business attire walked like they were on a mission. Her eyes fell on a man dressed in baggy jeans and flannelette shirt using the pay phone.

She longed for the comfort of her apartment. What wouldn't she give to be able to freshen up and be surrounded by her belongings? To cradle her bear, the last gift she'd received from her father, the last present before he did the unthinkable and disowned her.

Taking a deep breath in, she turned and walked resolutely in the opposite direction instead.

It was only six short blocks to Schultz's office. Ten, maybe fifteen minutes away if she were to get caught at a few red lights. She'd then be surrounded by some of the country's elite police force. Nothing could go wrong in that short a space of time.

Her hand in her bag, clutching her piece – just in case – Emily walked on high alert, looking straight into the eye of anyone approaching until they'd passed her.

Then Emily thought she caught something. She stopped in the middle of the footpath, only a few buildings into her trek. Moving her head down slightly, she turned her head around a little until her ear was above the back of her shoulder.

Out of the accompanying street noise, a set of footsteps stopped. She turned to scan the sidewalk. The only person who was not currently moving was someone using a pay phone. Emily assumed it was a man by his loose jeans, baggy jumper and a cap he was wearing reversed.

Tightening her grip around her gun, she continued walking towards the corner. The set of footsteps behind her returned. Out of the corner of her eye, Emily saw a cab approaching. She stepped to the curb and hailed it, and used the opportunity to glance back up the street. The pay phone was vacant and so was the sidewalk. The cab driver didn't slow down as he went past.

Stamping her foot, Emily threw her arm up in the air at the driver. Glancing over her shoulder, all she saw were busy business people.

The next intersection was only one building away. A group of people on the other side of the intersection were waiting for the signal to cross the road. Emily kept her focus on them and walked faster.

A red scooter was parked on the edge of the footpath. She looked over the handlebars. "Damn," she whispered. "No keys."

Picking up the pace, she continued towards the intersection. The footsteps behind her also picked up.

"Don't be silly. Keep your focus. Not long and you'll be safe, and this city can return to normality," she told herself.

The intersection was now within grasp. The group on the opposite side of the intersection was growing. Surely, some of them had to be going up her street.

A black van with heavily tinted windows slowed down and crawled alongside her. Emily pulled her piece up, until it was just below the seam line of her bag. A side door rolled open. Emily walked even quicker.

The van door slid fully open and out jumped its occupant. Emily's grip tightened on her gun as she felt her other arm being pulled behind her.

Turning around with her gun firmly in her hand, she thumped her attacker with its butt. The grip around her arm loosened.

Her back knee bent, Emily used the momentum of her spin to land in a defensive pose, her leading knee parallel with her toes. Clenching her gun, she pulled her arm back until it was next to her face, keeping the other in front of her body, ready to block any strikes.

In front of her, a man dressed fully in black staggered to his feet. He was only a little taller and more solid than her.

"Come on, get up. You've been sent to finish me. Have you not? Then at least try," she said through gritted teeth.

"Hurry up," the driver yelled.

Her attacker looked up as he worked on gaining his balance, a drop of blood blooming from the corner of his mouth. Emily's mind flashed back to the file with all the current personnel. She was certain he was one of them.

She refocused just as he lurched forward and stood her ground, unflinching.

He raised his arm, ready to make his move. His hand was a few centimeters from her face, and Emily was ready. She grabbed his attacking arm and pulled it behind him, and in a swift move she brought him down to his knees, her gun now pressed against his temple.

The man struggled but Emily's grip tightened.

"You'll only be warned this once," Emily yelled, looking between her attacker and the driver. "Next time I won't be so nice."

The driver raised his arms, and with a nervous twitch, he nodded.

"You heard me?" She pressed her gun farther into her attacker's temple.

He managed a small nod.

"I can't hear you!" Emily now had her attacker's face pushed against the pavement.

"Y-y-yes."

She slammed her gun handle into the back of his head. His body went limp.

Standing up, she pointed her gun at the driver. He slowly raised him arms again, looking nervously between her and his colleague, who was now out cold.

A couple of nearby pedestrians screamed, one of them rushing to pull out his phone.

Emily lowered her gun, brushed herself down, and walked away. She looked back at the crowd.

"Nothing to see here, people."

The group assembled by the intersection remained frozen, looking at her in disbelief. Ignoring them, she turned the corner and tucked her gun away at the small of her back in her jeans waistband.

Chapter 30

This road was a little narrower and quieter than the bustling Collins Street. The center tram lines were replaced with center horizontal parking spaces and the occasional scrawny tree with barely any canopy.

It won't be long and there'll be back for another go, Emily thought as she looked around.

Weaving in between traffic, Emily crossed to the other side. Her breathing came heavier now that she walked uphill. She pushed through, reminding herself that it was only five short blocks and she'd be safe.

Tires squealed as a black van drifted around the corner.

Emily was halfway across the intersection, and fully exposed.

"Crap."

She looked around. The only cover was an automated public toilet in the center island. Emily ran to it and pressed the button frantically to open the door. Peering back down the street, she saw the van was moving slowly, as if its occupants were looking for someone. For her.

The door finally opened and Emily slid in just as the black van slowly drove past her. She leant against the wall, getting her breathing back as the door closed.

The ringing tone on her phone echoed through the toilet. "Crap."

She looked at the screen. "Double crap."

"Lee," she answered.

"Lee, it's Schultz. How are you traveling?"

"Ah, on foot."

"You need back-up?"

"No, I'm fine. Can't really talk right now."

"Just checking. We've had calls filter through of a crazy woman kicking some butt down on the corner of Collins and Queens."

"That'll teach the prick to try and attach me from behind."

"Be safe."

"Always. You know me."

"When you get here, you do know there'll be paperwork you'll need to complete."

She shrugged. "Yeah. Self-defense."

"Just keep it to a minimal out there. Okay?"

She ended the call. Checking her settings, she ensured her

phone was now on silent.

Thump. Thump, thump.

Emily froze.

She could hear someone repeatedly pressing a button. Quietly she drew her gun, cocked it and aimed it at the door.

She pressed the button and the door began to slide open. Emily stood there, poised. Waiting.

Her gun still aimed, she moved towards the side of the open doorway. A startled little old woman stood before her.

Emily raised the index finger of her spare hand to her lips and the woman nodded. Stepping outside, she immediately looked both sides, her gun poised.

No one there.

She moved to the nearest corner of the toilet building. Nothing. Emily walked all the way around the small toilet block before returning to the old lady who'd remained standing there, frozen.

"Sorry." Emily placed her gun in her rear pants waistband.

The woman didn't say anything before locking herself in the toilet.

Emily was now alone. She didn't like this street. It was too exposed and didn't have enough places to disappear into. But it was the most direct route to Schultz.

Crossing the road, Emily felt her phone vibrate. She ignored it. It rang again. She pulled her phone out and checked the screen. The caller ID was a private number. She disconnected the call. They immediately rang back.

"You're not to call me," Emily answered, assuming it was

Sharon or Harry.

"Why not?" a man's voice with a thick Chinese accent asked.

"Who is this?" Emily demanded.

"Bank of Victoria. You know it?"

"Depends. Who's asking?"

"It's rigged with explosives."

"Impossible. That building is barricaded. Stop wasting my time." Emily moved her phone away from her ear.

"Tick Tock. Three hours and counting."

Emily returned the phone to her ear.

"What do you want?"

"You're going to pull out of your investigation."

"What investigation?"

"You know all too well what I'm talking about. It's littered all over your wall and your table."

Emily stopped walking, her full attention now on the call.

"You're causing quite a stir and bringing unwanted attention our way," the caller continued.

"Just doing my job."

"But this time you aren't, are you?"

Emily didn't reply. This assignment had been disregarded. Management apparently had more important assignments for her to work on.

The caller continued. "If you want to get through the next few hours alive, you'll hand over to us all of the information you've found."

"I highly doubt it."

"Behind you is a statue the locals call the bronzed rhythms of metropolis."

Emily turned around. She couldn't say she knew what that statue was called, never being one for understanding modern art. But it was a statue of some description.

"That's right. Beautiful, isn't it?"

"If that's your taste," she replied, looking around her.

She couldn't see anything or anyone that stood out besides a few vans parked in the center of the road. The rear ends of the vans were facing her.

"You're going to go around to the other side and take a seat."

"I am, am I?"

"There's a gun pointed at you."

Emily looked down and saw a red light pointed at her chest. She looked around, trying to visualize where the line of sight was coming from.

"That's right," the caller continued. "When you're seated you'll place everything you have on us between the hedge and the statue."

A few people, mainly men in business suits, walked past, all on their phones, absorbed in their own conversations.

"All the information I have is in the apartment."

"We both know that's not correct. We've seen your internet activity. Very sneaky but not sneaky enough for my computer guy." The caller paused. "You'll walk away. Don't look behind you. Do not — I repeat, do not — go to the police. We know how to find you."

The call ended but the red laser light was still pinned on her. With no choice, Emily walked towards the statue. A small circular garden was divided into quarters by hedges stopping at the base of the statue, with low-lying greenery planted between the hedges.

With the red dot still fixed on her, Emily sat down a little farther around than where she was meant to. From here she could see the intersection and the parked vehicles.

Emily assumed by how fixed the mark had been on her that the shooter would have to be positioned in a nearby vehicle.

Rummaging through her bag, her chest still marked, she pulled out a hard drive and placed it near the statue's base. Taking one last look around, she stood up and continued up Queen Street.

The mark was gone from her chest.

Chapter 31

Emily was now a block and a side alley away from the statue. Away from any direct traffic, Emily made a phone call. A phone call she hoped wasn't about to bring down one of the tallest buildings in Melbourne.

"Schultz," he answered on the second ring.

"We have a problem," Emily replied. "The Bank of Victoria is rigged."

"Yeah, there's been some shady business dealings happening there."

"No. I mean it's rigged with explosives."

There was silence on both ends of the line.

Breaking the silence, Schultz asked, "What do you mean?"

"Just had a call. I was ordered, at gunpoint, to leave behind all information I had on the Bank of Victoria, Andrew and the syndicate. I had to leave the hard drive."

"Did you?"

"What do you think? I had a marksman mark me during the whole ordeal."

Besides Schultz's chair squeaking as he rocked back and forth in it, the line was silent.

"How long do we have?" Schultz asked, his tone a lot more concerned.

"You're staying out of this. They've ordered no police. I'm not even meant to be contacting you."

"We can't just sit back here and twiddle our thumbs."

"I'll think of something. Just hang tight. I'm sure you've got plenty to keep you busy."

"Yeah, but that doesn't involve turning my back on a potential terrorist attack on the city."

"I'm a couple of blocks away. I'll be there shortly with the information I have. Promise me something."

"I don't know. It's not usually good when you do this to me."

"Keep this quiet. Just for the moment. Please," Emily pleaded.

"I can lose my job over this. You know that, don't you?"

"You and I can always go and freelance together. I'll see you soon."

Emily disconnected the call before Schultz could reply and hightailed it. Only two blocks left. Gun in hand, she began to run.

Approaching the last corner before Schultz's office, she heard gun shots behind her. Looking over her shoulder, she saw people screaming and yelling, running for safety in every direction. Emily took protection behind a thick concrete gate post and waited.

Two vans were traveling up the street, one on each side of the road. A white van on the far side and a black van in the lane closest to her.

They were tearing up the street with their bullets.

She quickly pulled out her phone and dialed Schultz's number. He answered on the first ring.

Gunfire resounding around her, she whispered into her phone, "You may want to get some uniforms out on the corner. NOW."

Before Schultz could answer, she hung up the phone, and as she put her phone away, she started counting. There was a pause in the gunfire. She turned in their direction and aimed. Her bullet found its mark. The rear shooter fell out onto the street.

The van was almost level with her. She fired at the front passenger window, and it shattered. The van was now level with her. She stared into the gun barrel of the passenger and fired. He fired at the same time, but Emily was already in motion. She ducked behind the cement post. Shards of cement flew past her as the bullet lodged in the post she was hiding behind. Cautiously, she peered around it. The passenger was slumped over the dash.

Emily fired two more shots, this time into the rear tire and fuel tank. Hiding behind her cement barrier, she braced her head. The van exploded. Her body was thrown forward, the explosion echoing through the street.

In the distance, sirens were growing louder. Emily peered around the corner again. The black van was up in flames. Looking up and down both sides of the street, she couldn't see the white van.

On guard, she entered the street and walked over to the shooter who lay on the ground. Her gun aimed at him, she kicked his gun out of his reach. He lay there, still.

"Stand back," a feint voice shouted from far away.

Her gun poised at the assumed deceased gunman she glanced towards the shout. Schultz was running towards her.

Her focus returned to the gunman. She looked closer at the face.

"Stand back." Schultz grabbed her arm and pulled her back.

"It's them," she said, still staring at the gunman.

"How do you know?"

"His record is on this." She pulled her actual hard drive from her bag and handed it to Schultz.

"I... I don't understand." He turned it over in his hand. "I thought—"

"You thought I'd hand over my information so easily?" Her eyebrow rose up. "Really?"

"I shouldn't ever doubt you."

"The hard drive I left them contained photos."

"Do I even want to know what type?"

"Just a hard drive full of unicorns, trolls, fairies and elves."

"You serious?"

Emily nodded.

"Love it." Schultz chuckled. "Focus," he muttered to himself.

"Protect it," Emily told him. "Bring justice to Harry and his fellow farmers. The corruption brought on by the syndicate and Andrew need to be brought to the public's attention."

"I'll get this forwarded."

While Schultz was talking with a fellow detective, his back turned to her, she picked up the dead gunman's gun and checked it. A few bullets left; enough to tide her over. While Schultz was still talking to his colleague, she searched the gunman. She found a few more rounds and snuck them into her pockets.

"Hey, what are you doin' there?" Schultz interrupted his conversation and turned her way.

Emily stood up. "Just tying up my laces. Don't want to trip up. The city is a dangerous place today."

She smiled as his gaze shifted between her and the body, and back to her.

"And you've always had that gun?" Schultz's colleague asked.

"A girl's gotta be protected."

"Is it even registered?"

"Promise is a promise. I'll be in touch," she yelled out to Schultz as she ran away from the fiery van.

Chapter 32

Emily's legs were tired and aching, but she was only four blocks from the Bank of Victoria headquarters. Gritting her teeth, she pushed on.

The city was still much the same, modern buildings still replacing the older ones, robbing it of its old-world charm. But one thing that hadn't changed in the city was the impact the concrete had on everyone's feet.

Emily felt her phone vibrate against her leg. She slowed to a jog and checked the screen. Private number, it said.

Swiping along the bar, she answered her phone. "Yeah."

"I should've shot you when I had the chance," a man replied, his accent thick, sounding similar to the one who'd called her earlier.

"Why didn't you?" Emily looked around; she was alone.

"You've got some fight in you."

"You would too if someone attacked you."

"Your family, how are they? Their hearts still beating?"

"Did you have something to do with it?" Emily kept walking.

"Innocent lives cannot be helped. They're casualties of war."

"You bastard."

"I've been called worse." His laugh was evil, sending chills down Emily's back.

The caller continued. "I'll take that as a compliment. That bullet was meant for you."

"How did you know where I live?"

"I have my eyes. Remember Brian? It's amazing what he can find."

Emily ignored the last comment. "How do you sleep at night?"

"Quite nicely, thank you for asking."

"The farmers. Their families. Their livelihoods. You've broken them."

"If they're broken after a little tussle, they were never going to make it through the long haul."

"Who made you god?"

"My investors. It's their interests I have in mind."

His accent was growing thicker, almost breaking into his native tongue.

"Don't you have enough cows in China?"

"The grass is greener on the other side of the fence."

Emily could hear muffled chuckles on the other end. Was she on speaker phone? Were there others in there?

"The last forced acquisition, that's what's going to trip you up," Emily yelled into her phone. "And I hope everyone with you there has heard that loud and clear."

Emily hung up the call.

She felt the anger grow inside her. Her cheeks were burning. She waved her hand in front of her face, trying to cool herself down, but it wasn't working.

Time was ticking away, quickly. She picked up her jog towards the city square when her phone rang again.

Answering it, she yelled, "Seriously? Where do you get off?"

"Lee? It's Schultz. You good?" She could hear the concern in his voice.

"Yeah." She stopped in some shade from a neighboring tree. "Just had another call from them."

"I'll get my people onto it again. See if we can find out anything."

"Not sure what use it'll be. They're using a private number."

"You'll be surprised what they can find."

"He confirmed my sister and niece were innocent casualties today. I was their intended target."

"Right. You need to go into protective custody. Now."

She heard Schultz click his fingers. He was probably directing them to listen in on the phone call or order them to track her number.

"No, I have a bombing to-"

Emily felt something grab her around her shoulders and pull her back.

"You're going to pay," she yelled at them as her arms were wrenched back.

Another man approached from the rear and shoved some fabric in her mouth then wrapped a length of material around her mouth and secured it at the back of head.

She kicked and swung her shoulders around but they pulled her arms back farther. In the commotion, she was able to slide her phone into her back pocket.

Her screams came out muffled.

The kidnappers pulled her backwards; it was all she could do to keep from tripping up with the speed they were dragging her.

With the next step, she felt herself being lifted higher than she was expecting. She landed with a loud thump on what looked like a van floor. Dazed, she lifted herself up onto all fours, noting with relief that her hands had not been tied back, but was kicked down by a masked man.

Three men huddled in around her and the van accelerated as they slid the door shut.

Speeding down the street, Emily tried to sit up but a boot connected with her stomach. Twice. Huddled over, her arm protecting her stomach, she tried to look up at her attackers.

A loud slap echoed through the van. Her head swung sideways and she felt her cheek warm.

Collapsing in a heap, she used the movements of the speeding vehicle to shuffle backwards until her back touched the van's wall and she could see their eyes poking through their balaclavas.

Every time the van hurtled around a sharp corner, Emily was thrown around the floor. Bruised and battered, she became disorientated after the first few corners.

"You going to be quiet back there?" the passenger in the front seat asked.

Her eyes apologetic, Emily slowly nodded her head.

He stared at her through the mirror for what felt like ages before he said, "Very well. Boys, remove her gag. Be careful, she might bite."

They chuckled. The one near her kept himself at arm's length away from her and untied her gag. Emily wiped her mouth on her top.

They traveled in silence, the turns becoming less frequent. *A highway or a major road,* she thought.

Emily eyed the door then the attacker sitting alongside the door, who was staring down at her. The corner of his lips was turned up into an evil smile.

"You're a fighter. Just like your daddy." He slid his leg in front of the door.

Keeping her eyes focused on him she swung her legs around, aiming for his head. A few centimeters from his face, her foot stopped. She was stunned. She went to move her leg again but the grip around her ankle tightened. Emily flinched before relaxing her leg.

Without a word, the other masked man pulled her arms behind her and she felt them being bound together.

"A fighter here, boss," he said as he finished tying her hands up.

The driver turned around and winked at Emily. One of his front teeth was missing. Emily wriggled and kicked the back of the driver's seat. The van swerved a little but the driver quickly straightened it up.

"Just like her father," the front passenger said as he looked at her through his rear-view mirror.

"You keep him out of this," Emily hissed.

"Does he know you're back in the country?"

Emily ignored him, turning her face away.

He chuckled. "That's what I thought. You two will be reunited shortly. I reckon he'll be impressed to see we've found his little daughter."

The other men looked at each other before forcing a chuckle at what he'd said. She assumed he was their boss.

"What do you want with me?"

"All in good time. All in good time, my princess."

Emily lowered her eyebrows and stared at him.

The driver nodded at one of the burly men in the back with her. He stood over her, blocking out what little sunlight was filtering in through the front window.

Then all went black.

When she regained consciousness, her face was against the van's floor and her head was thumping between her ears. She tasted blood when she licked her parched lips.

Emily lay there in silence, exhausted and in pain, with her eyes closed. She hoped either the trip or her suffering would all be over soon.

Chapter 33

The van came to a complete stop and the door slid open. Emily's body felt limp and sore, and she no longer had the strength to fight. They heaved her from the van and dumped her on a concrete floor, jarring her side.

"Get up," a gruff voice with a Central European accent demanded as he untied her bound arms.

Emily felt something small prod her in the back. A gun barrel? It was too narrow to be a boot.

Mustering every inch of strength left in her body, she tried to get up onto all fours. She wobbled there for a moment before collapsing back onto the cold concrete floor. Its coolness gave Emily a small reprieve from her suffering, but it was short lived. She received another prod in the back, this time stronger than the first.

"Get up."

Another prod.

Emily groaned, grimacing as she crawled up onto her hands and knees.

"You wanna end your life like your mother did? You stay there any longer and you will."

Emily recognized this voice. She turned her head towards it as she staggered up onto her feet.

"Uncle Fu?" Emily closed her eyes, grasping for air. "What... I don't-"

"Don't take it personally. This is business."

"Business? It's been..." Emily struggled through the pain in her chest to get a decent breath. "It's been... you... all along? Why?"

"Your father warned you back in Sydney. Have you not learned a thing?" Emily tried to reply but she was interrupted by Fu, who continued, "I told your father he should've been more forthright with his penalty towards you."

Fu walked slowly around her, looking her up and down while swinging an old clock on a chain. She counted the steps, three on each side, two across her front and feet.

He was now standing in front of her.

She looked up at him. He was studying his clock.

"The thing about you westerners. You value your possessions," he waved the clock in front her, "more than family."

Emily flinched but kept her mouth shut. She knew he was

fishing for a reason to display his strength.

Looking around, she noted three sturdy men stood around her. They were all armed, and their guns were aimed at her. Their stony faces were focused on her, waiting for any reason to pull the trigger. Their camouflage pants were tucked into calf-length laced boots. Their clothing and their stance, military-like. From her angle, Emily couldn't see if there were any emblems on their shoulders. Probably just wannabes.

Behind the armed men stood the three masked men who'd accompanied her in the rear of the van and the two in the front — the driver and the passenger.

"He always had a soft spot for you," Fu said. He paused but continued to pace in front of her. It felt like an eternity to Emily before he spoke again. "I don't know why he did. You're not even blood."

Emily spat a ball of blood-streaked saliva at his feet. Fu glanced down at his shiny black boots now splattered with spittle before looking back at her.

Before she knew what was happening, he landed a right fist across her jaw. Shocked, Emily staggered on her feet.

Holding the corner of her mouth, she ducked before the next blow could connect with her other side.

Fu stepped around her. Closing her eyes, Emily took a deep breath in, her chest screaming, and waited. In some distant corner of her mind, she was still hoping this was all a bad dream. It was insane to think that the biggest terrorist attack on Australian soil was the brainchild of her uncle.

She felt her uncle step behind her. She swung her legs out

from underneath her, grimacing as her palms landed on the concrete. Her feet connected with the back of his legs. Fighting through the pain, she mustered up all the strength and pulled his legs out from under him.

The armed men took a couple of steps closer, still on guard, waiting for Fu's command.

Fu groaned as he landed on the concrete face down. Before he knew what was happening, Emily had his arms pinned behind him.

"Get her," he yelled as he tried to wiggle himself free.

Emily stood her ground, her arms locked around his.

"You'll pay for killing my sister," she hissed into his ear. "That's right. It doesn't matter if you're blood or not. Family is family."

The three men stood around them, their guns still aimed at her.

"Get her. Now," Fu yelled.

The next thing she knew, Emily felt a piercing pain in her back. Her grip loosened and she fell to the ground. Gasping for air, she reached out for her uncle.

She must be dying, she thought as she struggled to get even the smallest amount of air into her lungs.

Fu spat at her, missing her face by a few centimeters.

"I'll let you live. For now."

He clicked his fingers at his armed men then again at Emily.

They moved in sync with each other. One kept his gun aimed at her while the remaining two grabbed her under her armpits, lifting her just off the ground.

Emily fought, wiggling her legs and shoulders. She received another thump across her back. Shards of pain sliced through her lungs like broken glass. She wiggled her arms to get free, but their grip tightened.

Chapter 34

Emily walked in silence from what appeared to be a disused warehouse into another open space, this time a little smaller, with new stainless-steel equipment installed — a production line of some sort.

The building was just as derelict as the room they'd left. Its windows were high up, way above eye level. They'd been blacked out, but she could glimpse some patches of sky through a few smashed ones. The only light came through the cracked or broken windows. In the center of the room sat a simple table with two chairs, one on either side.

They marched Emily over and slammed her into one of the chairs. Next, they handcuffed her arms and legs to the chair.

Emily wiggled but the chair refused to move. It was then

she realized the chair had been cemented to the floor.

The armed men once again took their places around her, their guns over their shoulders and their postures relaxed, with their hands folded in front of them as if protecting their family jewels. Turning her head was uncomfortable, and Emily flinched as a stab of pain shot through her neck.

At least she'd managed to establish her travel companions were nowhere to be seen.

Turning back around, Emily faced the other empty chair in silence. The only noise now came from a few pigeons who flew out of one of the broken windows.

After a while, Emily heard a few sets of heavy footsteps and something being dragged behind her. She tried to turn her head but she was in too much pain. Keeping her head straight, she clenched and unclenched her fists, waiting.

The three men surrounding her jumped at attention. Their chests were puffed, shoulders pulled back and their hands straight down by their sides.

Emily squeezed her fists closed, then opened them before closing them again.

Four more uniformed men marched past her and stopped in a diamond formation. Emily peered at the small gap in their middle but couldn't see past their broad shoulders. She looked down to their feet. Another set of legs, a lot smaller and frailer than theirs, was being dragged along the floor.

Two men stepped between the chair opposite her and the table. She couldn't see past them but realized they were cuffing someone to the chair, just like they had her. The guards were bent over, their arms and shoulders moving back and forth as they worked on restraining the other unfortunate who, Emily thought, was about to get the shock of their life when they came around.

Her neck still aching, Emily looked around the best she could manage. The armed men were still standing at attention. There wasn't any emotion on their faces as they stared down at her.

Turning back around, Emily saw the men surrounding the other chair step back to take their positions behind it. She recognized the one facing her directly. He was the driver.

A groggy moan coming from across the table brought her attention back to the occupant of the chair opposite her.

Emily studied the person. They were slender but with no muscle definition. Their hair was wild and short, and gray. She assumed he was a man by the structure of his hands. What clothing he had on him was torn and streaked with grease. He groaned again, and this time his head moved a little to the side before flopping back down.

"What on earth have you done to him?" Emily asked and looked around at the men surrounding her.

Little chuckles erupted from the four who had just secured the man into the chair, but she got no other answer.

Emily glared at one of them, and he quickly composed himself and stood tall and stiff, like all the others.

The room was silent again.

Emily returned her attention to the prisoner across the table. He was still groaning as if in pain, his head moving a little more freely from side to side. She tried to get a look at his face but she couldn't lean forward and his hair obscured his face completely, slumped as he was. The men behind her sniggered once or twice but she ignored them and concentrated on the man in front of her.

"Ah good, you're both here." Emily heard her Uncle Fu approach from behind her.

"What have you done to him?"

"A lot more than I've done to you."

The man opposite her became more responsive, almost agitated, when Fu spoke.

"You're a monster." She spat at the ground between her and Fu.

He looked down the end of his nose to her before a smile emerged.

"It's good to see you two finally reunited."

Chapter 35

Emily stared at Fu, puzzled.

Fu grabbed a handful of hair and pulled the man's head back. She gasped. "Dad?"

His face was a patchwork of different shades of blue, purple and black, and his good eye was swollen. He tried to open his eyelids but only the lid over his glass eye lifted.

"You mongrel," she spat at Fu. "You're lucky I'm wearing these bracelets." The handcuffs rattled against the arm rest as Emily tried once more to free herself.

Fu cackled, sending shivers down Emily's back. This was the uncle she'd grown up with. The loving and caring person who was always there when she felt alone. Who'd accepted her as one of their own when she was taken in by her adoptive parents. He'd now turned on his own brother, her father.

Emily quietened and stared at her broken father. The once strong man was now a worn and tired old man.

"It seems..." Fu stood behind Emily. She felt him breathing down her neck. He continued, "...you do find it hard to learn from any lesson that's dealt to you."

"You're going to be sorry."

A belly laugh erupted from Fu. "I'm going to be sorry." He breathed down her neck. "You'll be the one pleading with me by the end of today."

"I doubt that. You're just a weak man pretending to be strong. They're the strong ones. You're nothing without them." She nodded towards one of the armed men.

Fu's open hand connected with the side of her face. She hadn't seen it coming. Her head snapped to the other side, her cheek hitting the back rest.

"You're the one sporting a bastardized version of my family name."

She clenched her teeth until the pain subsided.

"Emily, stop. It's not worth it," her father softly pleaded.

"Only so there'd be no direct link to you."

She was a fighter and she wasn't about to quit. From a young age, her father had taught her to be a fighter, not to weaken in front of any opponent. She wasn't about to start now for her uncle's sake. She owed her life to her parents, to their sacrifices, and was determined to continue the big fight. Today was not going to be the day she lowered her standards.

"Your father has been too soft on you and your sister." Fu

stood behind her father now, looking down at him in disgust.

Emily's eyes were fixed on Fu, watching his every movement.

"After Sydney, he should've been more... How shall I put it?" He reflected for a moment. "More forthright in his punishment."

Fu looked at her. She caught a flash of disappointment on his face when he realized she wasn't biting.

"By the end of the day you will be giving me that hard drive. Otherwise..." He waved a device at her before placing it in the center of the table.

Emily's eyes widened with fear.

It was a simple timer with a countdown screen across the front and a green and red switch beneath. Emily also noticed a small button on the side facing her.

"You'll cooperate today. Otherwise your friend Harry will lose a lot more than just his farm."

The armed men's chuckles subsided when Fu scowled at the nearest one.

Emily fought hard to stop her built-up anger from exploding. Her fingernails dug deep into her palms as she fought for control.

"We'll see," Emily replied, her voice calm once her anger had subsided.

"No one is coming to save you. Well, they will, but you won't be alive to see it."

"So why wait? Get it over and done with. Shoot me NOW."

"All in good time. I want to teach you a little lesson first.

Every time you don't cooperate, or lie, I'll press this little button." Fu pointed to the side of the device. "Harry will be fifteen minutes closer to his fate. At the end of the day, I'm still getting his property."

"How do you sleep at night, killing innocent people?"

"They're not as innocent as you may think. Your sister. She was going to walk out on her husband. It wasn't because of another woman, like your sister thought. He'd been carrying out hits for us. While Harry... he's been fighting a gambling problem since the drought hit ten years ago. He was up to his eyeballs in debt."

She searched her father's eyes, looking for any indication of truth in Fu's words. She could see a slit of brown through the gap in his eyelids. Her father's head moved slightly, up then down.

Emily looked back to Fu. "How do I know you're telling the truth?"

"Trust. First lesson of the day. Do not question. Have trust in what you're told. Do not question everything you're told."

"Only if the source can be trusted."

Fu clicked his fingers above his head. She heard movement behind her.

"I trust you two have met before." Fu had his arm extended. Emily followed the direction his arm pointed.

Brian! Of course! Her eyes narrowed as he moved towards her.

Emily gave him a look of disdain and cleared the lump in her throat. "You could say that," she said to her uncle.

"Hi," Brian greeted her with a boyish smile. She ignored him.

Another table and what looked to be a couple of very comfortable computer chairs were placed perpendicular to theirs, and Brian set up his workstation. Out of the corner of her eye, Emily spied a couple of laptops, a printer, and a cordless keyboard and mouse.

The room fell silent as Brian set up his gear. Content with his setup, he nodded to Fu, who returned his attention to Emily.

"Brian has been a valued member of my team for years. He's been able to assist me with a lot of problems that we may not have been able to deal with so swiftly."

Brian's fingers flew over the keyboard. He wasn't paying any attention to them, his eyes fixed on the screens in front of him.

Emily's thoughts circled back to Fu's lesson and the concept of trust. *I trusted Brian,* she thought bitterly. Trust was something she was finding harder to do as her career matured. On many levels, corruption was rearing its ugly head. That was the problem you were faced with when you knew how to read numbers.

She no longer read the company financial write-ups in the media, unless required to do so for a case or a research project. They never told the full story. Only what investors needed to know — the top-level figures. What they didn't see were the under-the-table deals being made with corporations that may normally be perceived as conflicts of interest in the eye of the public and authorities.

"There was a lot of potential for you in our company," Fu said.

"I like being able to go to sleep at night with a clear conscience."

"Oh, I do, too. I love money. And lots of it. That is what makes me sleep easy at night."

"We're live," Brian reported, continuing to type.

"Good. Now for some fun."

"They'll be here," Emily said to him, suddenly desperate to buy herself some time. "Don't think for a moment you're going to get away with any of this. You'll rot in jail."

"Before anyone has a chance to find you, I'll already be in international waters."

Brian stopped and looked at Fu with a surprised look.

Emily studied the twitch in his eye; obviously this was news to him. The few men Emily was able to see didn't flinch at this news.

Sliding one of Brian's office chairs over, Fu plonked himself into it and rested his feet on the table in front of her. Picking up the device from the center of the table, he toyed with it, thinking.

"Question one. Why were you investigating the Bank of Victoria's land transfers?"

Emily opened her mouth to reply, but Fu interrupted her. "Think very carefully before you answer." His finger hovered over the small button on the side of the device.

The room was quiet, except for the keys being depressed

on the keyboard. Brian stopped and watched Emily, too, waiting for her reply. She was becoming uncomfortable with everyone staring at her, feeling like they were waiting to pounce on whatever she said next.

"It was a case handed to my boss."

Fu turned to Brian. With his palm facing towards the table, he moved his hand slightly from side to side.

"And?"

"And what? All cases come through my boss. He's the one who directs what cases I take on."

"Very well."

He held the device up, the numbers clearly visible to her. Two hours and thirty minutes remaining. Emily did some quick computing. It'd been approximately thirty minutes since she was told the bank headquarters had been rigged. Emily sighed, realizing it was going to be a very long afternoon.

Fu's finger moved towards the side button. Emily stared at the screen, waiting. She wasn't going to spill more than what was needed. Not at the cost of her client's confidentiality. Fu could threaten her all he wanted.

When he lifted his finger from the button, the number changed.

Chapter 36

Schultz paced the operations center floor, his hands on his hips, head bowed, thinking.

"Where are we with a location on Lee?" He looked around the room. Screens covered all the walls, and four stations with computer analysts typing away stood in its four corners.

"Working on it, boss," someone yelled from behind a screen.

Schultz had called in all the on-duty intelligence analysts and scoured Melbourne, looking for her. He had them tapping into everything — her phone, security cameras, traffic light cameras, anything that recorded any footage of her whereabouts.

"How long?" Schultz snapped.

"We're down to within a suburb."

"A suburb. What on earth have you lot been doing?"

"There's a lot going down in the city today. We're getting pulled in every direction. We're doing our best."

"Sorry. It's just Lee-"

"We understand. We don't want anything to happen to her either. We're doing our best."

"You look like you need a coffee," another analyst said as she looked up from her screen. "We'll call you the second we have something."

"No, I'll stay. Can't stomach coffee. Not right now, anyway."

Schultz walked over to a large screen that covered most of one wall. The screen displayed an array of images, newspaper and online articles, letters and typed notes.

"Xander, how are we going on the hard drive?" Schultz asked, his eyes not wavering from the screen.

Xander pushed his glasses up his nose as he walked over to Schultz, his baggy shorts flapping below his knees and his Hawaiian shirt hanging out. He tapped away at his tablet as he got closer.

"The information. It's mind-blowing. It's going to take us years for any of this to make its way through the court system."

"What do you mean?" Schultz looked at the screen, though he felt way out of his depth. He prayed the day would come when techies learned to translate their language so the layman could understand them.

"This is bigger than what you and I think. It runs deeper than just Harry's case."

"How deep?"

"Very. You'll be six feet under before everything on this device has been dealt with. Crikey, I'll probably be long dead before this is all done. And all this has links that lead to the Dark Web. This is huge."

"Good work. Keep going. I'm sure Lee will be adding to the workload before the day is out."

"Yes. I must see if she can teach me some of her kickass martial arts moves," Xander pondered loudly as he walked back to his station.

Chapter 37

Emily pushed back the pain. Every extra minute she kept it together was an additional minute Schultz had to find them alive.

Watching her father cringe as Fu chuckled, she felt her eyes swell with tears. She fought them back with happy thoughts from the times when she and her sister were younger. When her father was home they'd spend many days listening to their father's stories from his childhood in China. Safe in his strong arms, they sat still, listening, mesmerized by his tales.

"Why didn't you go into the family business? With your analytical skills and Brian's," Fu looked at him then returned his attention to Emily before continuing, "the family business could've reached new heights. New territories. You would've been set up for life."

Emily thought before replying. "I'm not one of you. Your words, remember?"

She felt the thud as the butt of the gun thwacked into the back of her head. Dazed, everything spinning around her, she pressed her back against the backrest and bit her lip. Her eyes closed as she pushed back the throbbing pain.

Her father let out a scream. She heard a thump and then he fell silent. She cracked open an eye to see his head slumped.

"You son of a bitch." Emily wriggled her arms and legs, forgetting the pain.

"Let's try this again, shall we? Have I not made the consequences clear to you?" He gestured towards the device.

It now flashed two hours and twenty-five minutes.

She couldn't tell Fu the truth; her father had been through enough torture by now. Any more could kill him.

"I'm developing my skill base," she said. Her heart raced as she kept her eyes focused on Fu, being careful not to blink.

"Skill base? I don't understand. Everything you need is here. We have our systems and procedures. They've served us well."

"I... I thought, getting a fresh perspective on how everything runs outside the family might be a good idea. Bring back some new techniques and expand on our current systems and procedures."

"Mmm." Fu thought for a minute. "You might be onto something there."

Emily smiled wearily. Her smile soon disappeared when she saw her father still out cold.

"Tell me something. Sydney. Why did you betray your family and your fellow community members?"

Caught off guard, Emily closed her eyes. She wasn't expecting this to rear its ugly head again. Choosing her words carefully, she replied, "To learn how they investigate, their tactics. So we can train our men to outmaneuver them."

Fu removed his finger from the device. Emily relaxed a little. She was still surrounded by armed men and a tech savvy nerd who could disastrously change her future at the click of a mouse.

Her phone vibrated against the chair. She lifted her hip up just enough for her back pocket to be off the chair so the noise wouldn't alert anyone. By the looks of them, no one had noticed. The phone vibrated four more times then stopped. A missed call. She slowly lowered her hip.

Emily looked skyward, silently thanking whoever was watching over her. She still had cell reception. Schultz and his team should be able to track her down. Emily felt a glimmer of hope. Soon this ordeal would be over.

"Boss." Brian looked up from his screens.

"What is it?" Fu snapped, annoyed to be spoken to when not warranted.

"Someone here, in this room, has a cell phone. I've just registered an incoming call."

"You sure? Everyone has been swept."

"Someone has been missed. The receiving end of that call

was in here."

Fu spun around and stared at Emily. She raised her shoulders, dropping them as her eyes pleaded her innocence.

He marched over to her and placed his gun against her temple. The cool metal sent a shiver down her back. Emily kept her eyes on her father, thankful he wasn't seeing any of this.

"Check her," he ordered, the gun pushing deeper into her temple.

Emily pushed back against the gun barrel.

Three men marched over. One supervised while the other two patted her down. Beginning with her legs, they felt in her shoes, her jeans legs before moving up and patting her. They stopped just before her chest and looked up to Fu.

"Keep going," he insisted.

Emily could see them hesitate but she gave them a small nod and they continued. She closed her eyes, wishing it would be over.

"All clear," one advised.

Emily opened her eyes. Both men were now standing in front of her, with the supervisor a step or two behind them. Fu studied her for a moment, looking her up and down.

"Check her pockets."

"We have, boss."

"Her back pockets."

The two guards held her arms while the one who'd been supervising unlocked her arm shackles. She was pulled up onto her shackled feet.

Emily wiggled, but their grip tightened until she stopped resisting. The man to her right reached for her pocket and pulled her phone out.

Fu slapped the side of her face. Too stunned to fight back, she dropped back into the chair and they quickly shackled her again.

Fu clicked his fingers and waved his hand, waiting for the phone. The men took their positions.

Phone in hand, Fu leaned over Emily. "Thought you could outsmart me?"

"Wasn't that hard."

"Let's see who it was." Fu turned her screen on. "Passcode?"

"Bite me."

"Here." Brian held his hand out. "I'll have this thing cracked open in a jiffy."

"Very well." Fu handed the phone to Brian while keeping his attention fixed on Emily. "Work your magic."

While Fu circled around her, Emily kept her eyes straight ahead. He'd take two steps then pause, then take a couple more. Standing between her and her father, he stamped his feet on the spot and stared down at her.

Still reeling in disgust with her uncle, she avoided his eye contact. Instead, she focused on a broken window in the distance. Anything to avoid seeing the evil in her uncle, the uncle she was once proud of.

"You're a real little tiger. This should make today... interesting."

Silence.

"We have something," Brian interrupted.

"What've you got?" Fu remained in front of her, unmoving.

"A number belonging to a," he looked back at his screen. "A Detective Schultz."

"The cops!" Fu slapped her other cheek.

Her face throbbed with pain, the heat from the repeated contact rising. Trying to drive the pain away from her face, she gritted her teeth and clenched her fists.

Fu walked over to Brian and grabbed the cell phone, placing it on the table alongside the timer.

"It won't be long," Emily said through a clenched jaw. "This place will be swarming with them."

Fu grabbed the timer and wiped thirty minutes off with one click.

Emily looked up at him, her eyes wide with shock, her mouth open.

"Don't worry, I've got it covered. When this timer reaches zero this place will go boom as well." Fu imitated an explosion with his hands. "With you in it. And as many of your friends as you've invited to the party. Whether you're dead or alive when it goes off depends on you."

Chapter 38

"Were we able to get anything, then?" Schultz turned to Xander.

"Yes." He typed away at his keyboard. "Yes, we did."

"And?"

Xander walked over to the big screens and tapped away on his tablet. A moment later an overhead photo of the city popped up. The image zoomed in from a bird's eye view to an overhead view of a suburb and the bay to the right.

Schultz stepped closer to the screen, concentrating on what was in front of him. "Where's this?" He pointed to the image of suburbia Melbourne.

"Just a minute."

The screen zoomed in further. Air conditioning units and

roof peaks became visible. The image moved a little farther south, and a shoreline and rows of boats appeared.

A red dot flashed on the screen.

"Don't tell me-" Schultz turned to Xander.

"Things just got worse. What you're looking at there is Melbourne's first sea port, now bustling Williamstown. Now, if I zoom in a little further you should see a boatshed butting onto the bay." He tapped his tablet. "I've sent the coordinates to your phone."

"Send them to all available personnel. Get everyone out there." His phone buzzed as he started stepping towards the door. "Also, send out the chopper and the dogs. Now."

Schultz paused at the door and looked back at Xander, who was busily tapping away at his tablet.

"Xander," Schultz called to him in his stern voice. He waited for Xander to look up, then, with a smile, he said, "Good job," and the doors closed behind him.

"Smith, White. With me," he ordered as he marched through the room full of detectives.

"What's up, boss?" short but fit middle-aged Smith asked.

Both men scrambled after Schultz, who was already waiting at the elevator.

"We have a ping on Lee. Check your phones."

On cue, their phones buzzed.

"We're off to the beach," White joked as he looked up from his phone, pushing his black-rimmed glasses closer to his eyes.

"It's going to be far from a picnic." Schultz wacked him over the back of his head.

White's glasses fell back down his nose. He pushed his glasses back up when the elevator doors opened.

"What do we know?" White asked as they took their places inside.

Schultz tapped the close-door button before turning to White. "We'll find out when we get there."

Chapter 39

Schultz plugged his earphones into his cell phone jack, placed one ear bug in his right ear and dialed Xander.

"Xander, talk to me," Schultz asked the moment the call connected.

"Okay, you're about ten minutes out. She's hasn't moved."

"Ten minutes! Put your foot down, White."

White planted his foot on the accelerator and the momentum pushed them all back into their seats.

"Make that five," Schultz returned to his phone call. "How's the surveillance in the area?"

"Sorry, boss, it's a dead spot. There's only the one camera next door, but that's facing into their yard."

"Shit." Schultz thumped his door panel.

"Chopper is about three minutes out," Xander advised.

"Okay," Schultz spoke in a calm voice. "Get them to stay back a bit. We don't want to spook them, not when there's open water at their back door."

"Before you go, boss... We've just lost signal to Lee's phone."

"You've got to be shittin' me."

White pushed the car further. Schultz held on while White swerved in between traffic, blaring his horn for anyone not getting out of their way fast enough despite their lights flashing and sirens blaring.

It was times like this Schultz didn't like traveling in undercover vehicles. The seconds ticked by slowly as they waited for cars to get out of their way.

"Right, stand by. I'm switching over to the earpiece."

Schultz unplugged his earphones and threw them to the floor before placing his ear piece in position and syncing it with his phone.

"You there, Xander?" Silence. "Xander?" he repeated.

"Receiving you loud and clear. You're less than a minute away. There's been no reported movement."

"How about out the back?"

Schultz listened as Xander spoke to someone in the background.

"Nothing there either."

"Let's hope we're not too late." With Xander still on the phone, Schultz turned his phone's screen saver on and tucked it away in his shirt pocket.

Looking out his window towards the bay, he spotted their chopper hovering.

"Too close," he whispered, shaking his head.

"What's your gut tellin' ya?" Smith asked as he sat forward in his seat.

Schultz let out a dry chuckle. "The facts are there's been no reported movements."

"Not since the boys have been up there. How about before?"

Schultz craned his neck forward. Police cars blocked off the street. White pulled to the side as he was directed by a uniformed officer.

The car was still rolling to a stop when Schultz hopped out. He checked his holster; still there.

"Schultz," he showed the local officer his credentials, "and White and Smith." They also flashed her their badges.

"Good. We've been here about ten minutes. There's been no movement," the female officer said, nodding at the detectives' identification.

"Okay." Schultz glanced up at the line of sheds converted to a variety of boating shop fronts.

"Second shed," Xander's voice came through on the earpiece.

Schultz moved his eyes to the second shed.

A simple roller door on one side and a double glass door with head-level windows on either side of the door. Corrugated iron requiring a fresh coat of paint adorned the front.

"Only the one entrance?"

"Yes, sir," the officer replied.

"How about the two side gates?"

"That side," she pointed to the side gate on the left side of the sheds, "is blocked. No way anything can get through all that crap. But there's a security gate to the right."

"Who controls that gate?" White asked.

"They do," she pointed to the last building, the one alongside the gate.

"Anyone spoken to them?"

"My partner is in there. Ah, here he comes."

A tall officer with a developing paunch stepped out of the shop. He glanced to the middle building as he walked directly to them.

"Pretrove, this is Detectives Schultz, White and Smith."

Nods were exchanged between them.

"Did you find anything?" Schultz asked, cutting the pleasantries.

"No one has been through those gates today, except for employees."

"Employees of all these?" Schultz swung his arm around, highlighting the neighboring buildings.

"No, just theirs."

"How 'bout the building in question?"

"A corporation took over a short-term lease two months ago."

Schultz stared at the buildings, thinking.

"The owner did say..." Pretrove had Schultz's full attention again. "They saw a group of people enter the middle shed a few hours ago. And they haven't seen them leaving yet."

"Do they have access to the bay?" Schultz asked.

"Yes. There's a marina out the back, and they've seen the tenants arrive and leave in a boat almost daily since they've taken on the lease. While I was in there, we checked their security cameras, and their boat is still docked."

"Good. We need to get the rear of the sheds covered." He directed the order to White and Smith before continuing, "Up above isn't going to cut it. Not with these guys."

"What do you need us to do?" the female officer asked.

"Just stay here and keep the traffic away. Pretrove, is it?" Before Pretrove could reply, Schultz was giving more orders. "Evacuate all neighboring buildings. Get them well out of the control zone."

"You think there could be something big about to happen?" Pretrove asked.

"Don't underestimate these people," Schultz replied.

"Geez, we don't usually get these people out here in the 'burbs."

Schultz raised an eyebrow. Pretrove took the hint and quickly walked across the street.

Schultz returned his attention to the middle building. "Just hope we're not too late."

Chapter 40

Emily kept her eyes focused on Fu as he circled around her limp father. His gun pointed at her father's head while the other hand held the timer.

Her body was covered in numerous bruises and cuts, and while she was unable to see her own face, she knew it must be inflamed. Her lips and cheeks felt puffy, and she was unable to see out of one eye.

But she was able to see her father's chest rise as he inhaled — not a lot. Just enough to know he was still alive. She couldn't stand losing the last of her family, all on the same day.

"Don't worry, Emily S, your father is still alive. Only just." An evil laugh erupted from deep within Fu's belly.

Emily's eyes narrowed as she glared at him. "Emily S?"

"Yeah, you heard me. You're stripped of the family name. You don't deserve it, not after continuously betraying the family."

"S?"

Her father stirred. Fu stopped behind him and pressed the gun to the back of his head.

"They were my same thoughts when I saw your adoption papers. What parents give their child a single-letter surname? Pretty pathetic, if you ask me. You're not even a legal citizen."

Emily clenched her fists and pulled on her cuffs. After all her attempts, she'd only made a few indents into the arm rests. Her wrists were another story. They had taken the full brunt of the torture and were streaked with weeping wounds where the handcuffs had cut into her skin.

Emily had known all along she'd been adopted, but that was all she'd been told. It was all she wanted to know. She didn't care who'd given birth to her. All she cared for was that her adoptive parents treated her as if she was one of their own blood.

"I don't believe you. I don't believe anything that comes out of that trap of yours."

"Brian, show her."

Without a word, Brian walked over to her, tapping away at a tablet. He presented her with a birth certificate.

It looked like hers.

"How do I know this is real? Anything can be forged these days. I'm sure Brian could've easily done that." She glared at

Brian.

Brian shifted uneasily, not making eye contact.

"Thank you, Brian. If she can't be gracious..." Fu nodded to Brian before turning to Emily. "I thought you'd want to know who you really are before you die."

"Oh, I know who I am. I don't need a piece of paper to tell me that."

"We all need to know where our roots are. And yours aren't in this family."

"As you keep reminding me. If I'm such a disgrace to your family name, why don't you just kill me? Get it over and done with. Come on. You know you want to."

Fu held up the timer. It now showed forty-five minutes.

Emily's hopes were dwindling fast. She knew she needed at least twenty minutes to get back into the city, and then she needed time to locate the bomb, and more time for defusing it.

Emily felt the barrel of Fu's gun press against the back of her head. She closed her eyes and the room fell silent. Even Brian's soft tapping on the keyboards faded away. Emily kept her eyes closed, waiting.

With her other senses blocked out, her hearing was sharper. In the distance, she could hear the faint rumble of a hovering machine. Still a way off, but not moving. A helicopter.

The barrel moved away from the back of her head. She let out a small breath of relief through her nose, still on alert, as they wouldn't have moved too far away. Probably getting ready to kill her now.

Behind her she heard metal being screwed onto metal. A silencer? She grabbed the arm rest and looked at her father.

Sorry, Dad. I'm so sorry for everything I've brought to the family. I love you, Dad. Please don't forget that.

Her father stirred, groaning in pain. A single gunshot echoed through the shed. Instinctively, Emily closed her eyes, bracing herself for the impact.

A few seconds passed with no pain. Her eyes swung open. She looked herself up and down. No blood. Nothing.

In front of her, her father's head stooped. Fresh blood poured down his shirt.

"You bastard," Emily screamed, tears streaming down her face.

"It was long overdue. He was always the weak one. Even our father saw him as the runt of the family. He was ashamed Tao shared the same DNA as him."

"He didn't deserve this."

"We often believe we don't deserve things. I'll leave this with you."

Fu placed the timer on the table, the seconds ticking away.

"Everyone," he clicked his fingers over his shoulders. "Time to move out."

"Don't think you'll get away with it that easy."

Chapter 41

"Gun shots, guns shots," Schultz yelled into his handheld radio. "Move in, now."

Around him, heavily armored officers moved in. Schultz stayed by the vehicles and watched. The officers rushed over quietly, their knees slightly bent, guns poised, ready. They were about five meters from the shed... Two meters... Everyone was in place.

Silence fell over the radio.

Schultz silently mouthed "Three, two." Then in his radio, "Now."

One group of men stormed the front door and another set forced the roller door open. They were all in.

Schultz held his breath. He wiggled at his collar and wiped

his forehead. Without a cloud in the sky or breeze off the bay, the sun beat mercilessly down on them.

The helicopter moved into position near the water's edge, a sun glare from one of its windows blinding Schultz. He shielded his eyes until the chopper moved slightly.

As the daze disappeared, he was now able to see the armed officers with their guns pointed at the shed, waiting.

"All clear in the front room," a scratchy voice came over the radio.

"No movement on the water," another voice reported.

Schultz kept his eyes on the building.

"All clear, boss," a voice over the radio said. "We have one deceased."

"Shit. Come on. Let's see what we can find."

The armed uniforms moved in first, their guns sweeping around the room. White and Smith followed Schultz towards the boat sheds.

"And one alive."

Schultz's step quickened, the other two detectives almost jogging to keep up. He stormed past the men sweeping the area one last time. Schultz, White and Smith pulled their guns out, ensuring they were loaded and ready to go.

"Eyes out. You just never know." Schultz paused outside the roller door.

It had been a few months since he'd completed his last sting, but he knew it was nothing compared to what they faced today. His usual stings involved drug manufacturers and dealers, and the worst they'd experienced were some unstable concoctions and gunfire. But those were visible and the locations had been well monitored. They knew exactly what they were going into.

Here, he had no idea. The unknown was making him feel anxious.

White and Smith nodded.

"We're coming in," Schultz reported into the radio.

He scanned the room. It was devoid of any furnishing. The only thing in the room was one van. Schultz signaled White and Smith, who swept around the van.

From the front of the van, White whispered into the radio, "Still warm."

"All clear." Smith signaled to Schultz.

Schultz motioned for them to move towards the only other door at the rear of the room. Standing either side of the door, White and Smith both nodded at Schultz, who slowly opened it. They moved in first, their guns sweeping around. Schultz was right behind them.

His eyes fell on the two chairs and table in the center. One occupant he could only see an arm of, but the other person was slumped in their chair and covered in blood.

Seeing their men surrounding the victims, the armed officers lowered their guns.

"Schultz?" Emily turned to look at him.

"Lee. Shit, look at you." He ran over to her side. "Get her out of these things." He rattled the handcuffs. "Now."

"It's okay. We have bigger problems than these bracelets."

Schultz followed her gaze to the center of the table.

"Forty minutes till what?" He reached for the timer, looking sideways at the cell phone alongside the device.

"I wouldn't touch it," a nearby officer advised.

"Why?" He looked between the officer and Lee. "Is that phone a detonator?"

"No, that's my phone, and according to my charming Uncle Fu, it's connected to a bomb. Or maybe several. Both here and at the Bank of Victoria HQ. The button your finger is hovering over reduces our time."

Schultz looked around the room.

"Where is your uncle?"

"They made an exit out the back somewhere. Behind the machinery." She gestured with her head towards the rear of the building. "Just before you guys stormed in here, I heard a splash and a motor."

"Smith." Schultz moved his head towards the rear of the building.

Without a word, Smith swept around the machinery and was out of sight.

"Shit. How many are with him?" His attention was back on Lee.

"Can I have my phone back?" She nodded towards the table.

"I'll need to take it in for evidence. You know, fingerprints."

Lee raised her eyebrow and repeated, "I want my phone. Wrap it in plastic if you must but I want my phone back."

Schultz nodded to someone behind her and a moment later

an officer was placing her phone inside a labelled evidence bag and handed it to Schultz.

"This isn't leaving my eyesight." He held it out towards Lee.

"Yep, whatever."

Schultz hesitated for a moment before placing it on her lap.

"We have some water movement," a crackled voice reported over the radio.

Schultz noticed Emily's posture tighten before she replied. "Fu, Brian and a few armed wannabe soldiers. About eight, from what I could see. Some were behind me." Tears began rolling down her cheeks and her hands were trembling.

"Get her a blanket and get her off that damn chair," Schultz demanded as he grabbed his handheld radio. "All eyes on the water. A watercraft escaped with approximately eight to ten occupants in it. They are deemed to be armed and dangerous."

"We need cutters inside. Now," White announced over his radio.

"Do you know anything about their craft?" Schultz asked Emily.

"Sorry." She shook her head. "They... they only left seconds before you guys entered. Please tell me you can find them. That bastard killed Dad in cold blood. I'm gonna make him pay."

"No, you won't. This time you'll be leaving it up to us," Schultz ordered.

"You know that isn't going to happen."

"Don't move and this won't hurt," a deep voice behind her

advised; she assumed it was one of the officers.

She felt the restraints tighten around her left wrist and flinched.

"Sorry," the officer said.

He released a small grunt and then she heard the sound of metal breaking. The tension around her wrist loosened. Pulling her hand around, she rotated her wrist one way then the other. The next wrist was freed and she did the same, getting the movement going in both of them.

"Right now, we need to get you looked at." Schultz wrapped a blanket around her.

"No, right now we have a few bombs to detonate safely." Emily grabbed her evidence bag-wrapped cell phone and leapt from her chair.

She paused by her dads' body. He'd been unshackled and laid on the ground, a white sheet draped over him.

"Smith, White. You stay here. Sweep the place. We need to find that bomb."

"Find a bomb. Since when are we the bomb squad?"

"Since they won't get here in time. It's up to you guys. You've got just over half an hour."

Smith moved forward to argue but White pulled him back. "Be safe, boss. Lee."

"Are you all right?" Schultz asked her. "You don't look too good."

"I'll be fine. I've been through worse. We've got a job to do, and we don't have much time."

"Thirty-four minutes, boss," White yelled as they exited

the room.

A crackled voice over the radio caused Emily to freeze. "We have a visual. I repeat. We have a visual."

Chapter 42

The mayhem above was replaced with silence as their craft plunged through the shallow depths of the bay's seabed. Everyone held their breaths. Fu sat next to the control seat, his knuckles white, expecting at any moment to come under attack.

They were within a meter from the seabed when Brian flicked on a set of dim headlights, not enough to light up a highway with but enough for them to navigate a short distance in front of them.

Fu checked their location on the GPS. He gestured with his hands to slow the vessel. Brian nodded and the craft began to slow. They were barely moving along.

Fu checked his watch. Five minutes had passed. Everyone

should be on the lookout for them. The sky would be busy, and police boats wouldn't be far from being deployed.

A small wry smile appeared on his face as he thought that no doubt he'd now be making his debut on Melbourne's Most Wanted list. He wondered what photo they'd use.

Checking a few settings, Fu ensured they were still undetectable. They were very close, but a lot could happen in the next few minutes that could spoil everything.

He sat back in his chair and closed his eyes, although his shoulders were still rigid. He was dozing off when he felt a nudge in his side.

Opening his eyes properly, he noticed Brian was pointing to the GPS. The two red dots nearly matched up.

Fu sat up in his chair, pulled the GPS off its brace and zoomed in on their location. He motioned for Brian to slow down. Brian eased off the throttle.

The markers were nearly aligned. Fu held his thumb and index finger about an inch from each other. Brian slowed their vessel down further. They were barely moving now.

Fu zoomed on their location further. He held up his hand flat. Their vessel stopped.

He placed the GPS back on its brace and looked at Brian, who was now sweating bullets. Fu raised his eyebrows and widened his eyes.

Pitch black was replaced with navy as Brian's trembling hand raised their vessel towards the surface.

They all turned their heads up, waiting.

"Slowly," Fu whispered. The first words he'd spoken since

they embarked the vessel.

Brian slowed their ascent.

Thump.

They stopped. A few nervous chuckles erupted in the rear. Fu held his hand up and everyone was silent. He listened. Nothing.

Fu lifted his open palm and Brian raised their vessel as Fu flicked a switch to his side. *Thump.*

Above them mechanics whirred, and they heard five clicks. Silence.

Fu's cell phone beeped. The notification on the screen read: Secure.

"Kill it," Fu said to Brian.

Brian turned everything off, including their motor and lights. The small whir of their fan confirmed that was the only thing still running.

A few jerks back and forth, then they were moving forwards.

One of the men behind Brian leant over and held his opened palm up for Brian to high five him.

Fu looked at him and he shrunk back to his seat.

"We're not out of the woods," he whispered. "We've still got at least two hundred nautical miles ahead of us until we can begin celebrating."

Everyone stopped and looked at Fu.

Fu continued at a whisper, "Once that hatch is released, we'll be able to stretch our legs. Until then we need to hang tight."

A few moans came from the back but Fu ignored them.

"That girl is going to pay." He turned to Brian, whose cheeks began to flush. "You're going to be busy, Brian. No one thinks they've won against me and believe they can get away with it."

Chapter 43

"Xander, get a bomb squad to the Bank of Victoria HQ, Collins St. We're on our way there now," Schultz spoke into his ear piece.

"Bomb squad? Okay. All bomb squad personnel not already on duty are being called in. Two bombs in one day. Busy day out there?"

"Understatement of the century. While you're there, see if you can locate the blueprints to the building."

"Okay. Am I looking for anything in particular?"

"Anywhere a bomb can be planted," Emily interrupted.

"Ah, Lee. It's good to hear your voice."

"Yours as well, Xander."

"And if you can get us clear traffic all the way through, it'd be appreciated," Schultz added. "We've got about half an hour before the whole block becomes a rubble heap."

"Consider it done. Green lights all the way through."

Schultz disconnected the phone call and side-glanced at Lee. She was strapped into the passenger seat, still wrapped in the blanket, staring out towards the city skyline, the sun soaking into her cheeks.

"Ever defused a bomb before?" Schultz asked.

"Huh?" Lee stirred in her seat.

"Bomb squad may not be there when we get to the bank. We've had to call extras in. It'll take time for them to assemble."

"Shit. You've got to be kiddin' me. I've seen it done in movies, but that's the closest I've come to a bomb."

"Excellent. Hopefully, we'll live to see the moon rise tonight."

"Your optimism is comforting. Thanks." Lee managed a small curl of the corner of her lips.

"And if we do... I'll get the drinks tonight. We're going to need them."

"Thanks, but a nice hot bath is calling my name." Emily closed her eyes and smiled as she thought about the warm water enveloping her.

"Mmm, is that an invitation?"

Her eyes snapped open. "No." She sat upright and pushed the blanket off her. "Any news on Unc- I mean Fu?"

"One drink?"

"Fu?"

"There's been a citing but it wasn't them."

"So he's still out there, somewhere?"

"I'm afraid so. I think now would be a good time for you to reconsider protective custody."

Lee chuckled. "You're not going to quit asking, are you?"

"Nope. Not until you agree."

"But we won't be able to work together again. My career... I'm starting to go places with it."

"And what price is your career costing you? You've been kidnapped today, and in Sydney, a few months back. Who knows where else you got yourself in trouble that I'm not aware of?"

"I'm a big girl. I know how to look after myself."

"He's a dangerous man, and now, with Tao out of the way..."

"It's a good thing my assignments take me around the globe."

Schultz stared out at the road in front of them. The suburb streets were quiet thanks to Xander giving them right of passage.

The road curved around, and it wasn't long until the skyscrapers enveloped them.

Unable to let the earlier discussion die, Schultz asked, "Is your career worth it if you're either dead or on the run?"

He flexed his knuckles as he anticipated the onslaught of city traffic.

"I've worked so hard to get where I am."

"We'll be able to get you into a position where you can still be doing the same job."

"It won't be the same. My career... I've shaped that myself. Sacrificed a lot. I'm not about to let all that go by the sideline and have a new career and identity handed to me. A career I'll probably hate with a passion."

"Please." Schultz placed a hand on her knee and moved his hand up and down her leg, trying to comfort her. "At least think about it."

A phone rang. Schultz pulled his hand back quickly and checked his cell.

"Umm... not mine. It's got to be yours."

Lee looked at her phone through the evidence bag. It kept ringing.

"Put it on speaker," Schultz said.

"How am I going to do that while it's inside this bag?" she waved it in front of Schultz. "You do know we have touch screen phones now, yeah?"

Before Schultz could say anything, she was already ripping the evidence bag apart and pulling her phone out.

The ringing stopped.

"Now you've tampered with the evidence." Schultz rolled his eyes.

The phone rang again.

"Yeah," Lee answered as she put the call through to her phone's speakers.

"Well... You're still alive."

Lee turned to Schultz, who gestured for her to keep talking.

Lee cleared her throat. "Of course. Why wouldn't I be?"

"Tick tock. Hope your boyfriend likes dark places. You'd better buckle up. The ride's about to get rough."

The call ended.

Lee's cheeks turned a little red.

"Dark places?" Schultz asked. "Do you think-"

"I'm exhausted. I don't know what to think anymore. He's probably trying to get me to react."

"We're nearly there. Do you think he's referring to where the bomb is?"

"Schultz. I honestly don't know what to think. I don't even know who or what kind of animal Fu is anymore."

Schultz caught a glimpse out of the corner of his eye.

"Hold on," he yelled as he raised his arm in front of his face.

Lee looked out her window. "What on earth is that-"

"Brace yourself," Schultz yelled.

A loud metal scraping sound pierced their ears as they were rammed from behind and their car spun around. They felt contact from the rear again — someone was pushing them into the intersection and the path of oncoming traffic. The rear windows shattered. Schultz tried straightening the car but the force from the collision drove them off course, heading straight for a traffic light post.

Schultz looked out of his rear-view mirror and saw a white van locked onto them. He turned his steering wheel so they pointed in the direction they were traveling. Their car began to turn towards an empty lane. He put his foot down on the accelerator and, just before they hit the post, they broke free from the van and sped down the empty lane ahead of them. A loud smash echoed behind them as the van collided with the traffic light post.

"One of Fu's mates?" Schultz asked, checking his mirrors.

"No idea." Lee leant forward and checked her side mirror. She sat back in her seat. "Yeah, it looks like it. They jumped me earlier but I sorted them out."

"Clearly, they wanted a rematch."

"Yep." She turned in her seat to check the damage to their vehicle. "Hope White didn't want his car back in one piece."

"Well, technically, it still is in one piece."

"Smart ass. I don't think they're going anywhere anytime soon."

A loud bang, and their windshield shattered. They ducked and the car swerved. Oncoming drivers blared their horns. Schultz quickly straightened the car.

"They've both got guns. Here comes another one," Lee said, looking out her side mirror. The two men were standing outside their van, guns aimed at their car.

Shultz pushed the car faster. Another bang, which hit their rear.

"You've really pissed them off today," Schultz said, checking his mirrors.

"Forget them. Get us to the bank. Our time is running out."

Chapter 44

They were navigating suburbia Port Melbourne, staying off the major roads, when Emily's phone rang again.

"Unknown number."

"Answer it," Schultz said.

"This had better be good," she said as she took the call.

"You're still alive."

"Fu. Nice try back there."

"They weren't my best men. I mean, they got their asses handed to them by you twice in one day now."

"What do you want?"

"Am I on speaker?"

"Why? What does that matter?"

"Put me on speaker. I want to talk to your boyfriend."

"What makes you think he's here with me?"

"My men have been following you two since the boat shed."

Emily looked out their rear window.

"What's up?" Schultz mouthed to her.

Placing the call on hold, she said quickly, "It's Fu. You noticed anyone following us since the boatshed?"

He checked his mirrors. "Yeah. You see that car two spaces back? It keeps weaving from one lane to the other?"

Emily checked her side mirror.

"He's doing it again."

"Black SUV?"

"That's them."

She took Fu off hold.

"You need to change your on-hold music."

"Not my problem. What do you want?"

"You're going to calmly hop in the black SUV that's a few cars behind you."

"And if I don't?"

"I'm not asking. You will be joining me as we take the family company global."

"Bite me. Not long ago you cast me from the family and shot my father. You were going to be a one-man show. Why the sudden change in tune?"

"I've had, I mean Brian and myself, have had some time to reflect on my treatment towards you. All I've wanted was for you to join the leadership team of the company. You've been fighting me every step of the way."

"There's a good reason for that. I'm my own woman. I do

my own thing and on my own grounds. You pull that SUV back, and we'll go about our own lives and leave each other alone."

"That won't be possible. With your father gone and no direct descendants, you're next in line to inherit his share of the business."

"I don't want it. You can have your stinkin' share."

"I still need to see you. You'll need to sign your share over."

"Unbelievable. My father isn't even cold yet and you're after his share."

"Business is business. It doesn't stop for anyone."

"You missed your chance, Uncle. You had me there and you forgot the paperwork. Rookie mistake. You should sack the admin guy. Where are you anyway?"

Emily turned to Schultz, who was on a call.

"Keep him talking," he whispered to her.

"Don't you worry about that. Tell lover boy there to get off the phone before Brian disconnects his call."

She turned to Schultz, her eyes wide open. "Hang up," she told him.

He raised his eyebrows and shook his head.

"Xander, you there?" He tapped his cell phone screen. His home page lit up. "Damn cell reception."

"No, it was Fu and Brian."

"Where are they? Tell him he's made it onto Melbourne's Most Wanted list."

Emily returned to her call.

"Send the required papers to my apartment. I'll get them

back to you."

"You don't get it, do you?"

"Get what?" She checked her side mirror. The black SUV was now directly behind them, about two car spaces between the SUV and their car.

Emily pulled at Schultz's arm and pointed her thumb towards the rear of their car. He looked and nodded then gently applied the accelerator.

"I don't owe you anything," Emily said into her phone. "I've only got me to worry about now. So whatever game you're playing, you can quit while you're ahead."

"I'm ahead, am I? Glad you finally realize it. I'm way ahead of you. Just remember one thing."

"What's that?" Emily rolled her eyes.

"I may not be there, but my eyes are. Don't think I'll be making your trip to Andrew's office a smooth one."

The call disconnected.

"What on earth was that all about? And who are those guys behind us?" Schultz asked, his voice now showing hints of anger.

"No idea," Emily replied, her head bowed.

"Lee, what aren't you telling me? I need to know what's going on."

"Let's just get to the bomb before it goes off."

"And those guys?"

"They've been following us since the boatshed. They're not going to be going anywhere anytime soon. Those clowns are after me."

"And your unc – I mean Fu. He won't stop at anything until he gets what he wants?"

"That's roughly it. Apparently, with my father and sister dead, my father's portion of the company gets handed to me."

"That's big. We could use that to bring him in." He rubbed his chin as he thought.

"Don't go there. I don't want anything to do with that scam of a company."

Sitting back in her seat, Emily adjusted her side mirror until the black SUV appeared in it. Less than two cars' length separated them now.

"Want to see if we can shake them?" Emily asked, keeping her eyes on their companions.

"I'd be delighted to." Schultz slowly pushed the car faster.

He turned at the next corner, into a narrower suburban street. Cars were parked on either side, making it almost a one-way street.

Halfway down the block, on cue, the black SUV turned into their street.

"Punch in the address for the bank headquarters." Schultz pointed to the GPS system. "We'll try to shake them but we need to make sure we're still heading in the right general direction."

He made another turn, into a just as narrow street.

"I don't have a good feeling about these narrow streets. We need to get back on the main roads."

Emily pulled the system off the suction cup and typed in the bank's address.

"No, that's not going to work. It's almost rush hour. The traffic will be building up."

The GPS accepted the address and started calculating their new route. Emily was placing it back on the suction cup when her phone vibrated.

It read: 1 new message.

She tapped it and a photo appeared.

The red illuminated numbers glared at her.

"What is it?" Schultz tried to look over her shoulder.

"Obviously Fu is not playing nice." She held her phone up.

"Are you sure that's legit? He did leave a device like that back at the boatshed."

Chapter 45

Looking between her phone and the expected time of arrival per the GPS calculation, Emily began to feel a glimmer of desperation.

"I don't care about those clowns behind us. Right now, we need to get out of here and back towards the city. If we don't, we'll be sifting for bodies in the rubble."

"I'll shake them first."

"You've been trying that and they're still sticking to us. We need to forget about them and get out of here. Now."

"Just a moment."

Emily looked in her side mirror. Schultz had turned into a parking space positioned between two shops, not far from the bustling South Melbourne markets.

"What on earth are you doing?"

"Getting them off our tail."

Reversing their car into the second to last car parking space, nestled in between a car and a van, he turned the ignition off and sat back in his seat, his eyes on the road.

Emily's heart raced. "This had better work."

"Have some faith in me, will you? They shouldn't be able to see past that van. See? There they go."

The black SUV drove past slowly.

"You sure?"

Schultz pulled out his phone and dialed Xander's number. His phone beeped at him and displayed a message: no signal.

"Seriously, no reception? Lee, you got signal on your phone?"

Emily unlocked her phone and checked her home screen. "Full reception."

"Fu must still have my phone blocked. Can you call Xander and put him on speaker?"

Emily dialed his number and he answered on the first ring.

"You've called to book me in for my Kung Fu class?"

"Muay Thai, thank you, and no, we've kind of got a little bit more important things on our hands right now."

"Yes, I can see that. Why are you guys still over on the South side of the river? You should've nearly been at the headquarters by now."

"We've just removed our heavy load."

"Good. You need to hightail it."

"Xander," Schultz yelled over from the driver's seat. "Lee,

put it on speaker."

She nodded to Schultz as she did it.

"Xander, can you ping Fu from Lee's phone? He's been making calls to her phone."

"I'm not liking my chances. He's a cunning man, that uncle of yours, Lee."

"Don't go there," she replied.

"Just see what you can do for us."

"I'll see what I can find, but my most likely chances of pinging his phone will be when he calls again."

"If he does," Emily answered.

"Also, looks like our time has been shaven by ten minutes," Schultz advised.

"O-kay. And we know this, how?"

"We're not sure if there's a second detonator. Lee received a photo not too long ago, with the countdown timer on it."

"Same one?"

"Looks very similar."

"You can't take any chances. You need to hope you've lost your heavy load for long enough to get yourselves to the building."

"We should be about ten minutes out." Schultz looked at the GPS to confirm.

"That's cutting it fine," Xander replied.

"Tell me about it. We'll need to have one or two of you guys keep an eye out on the waves for any chatter from Fu or any of his men. One of them will have to be talking about today sooner or later."

"Will do. I've got you guys up on the monitor now. I'll give you a clear run into the city."

"Only as we're approaching. Quiet streets will draw our heavy load, and they'll find us in a matter of minutes," Emily spoke up.

"Did you manage to find a copy of any blueprints for the building?" Schultz asked as Emily was about to hung up.

"Yes. It was well hidden but I've got a copy from five years ago."

"Let's hope it's still current. I need all the available analysts on this. You guys need to locate all the dark places in the tower."

"All the dark places?"

"Yes. We believe that's where the bombs are located."

"Do you know how many floors there are?"

"You'd better get going, then. Start from the bottom and work your way up. Also, see what cameras point at the building. We might score it lucky and catch them red-handed."

"Yes! I should then be able to see where and when they've entered the building and then again when they leave. From there I'll have the length of time they're absent from the camera and I'll be able to determine roughly where the bomb could've been planted."

"Get to it. I'll be back in touch as we arrive. Oh, and Xander?"

"Yeah."

"You've got about six city blocks, and these streets had

better be cleared." Schultz signaled to Emily to disconnect the call and applied pressure to the accelerator pedal.

They drifted around the corner and entered the outskirts of the city square boundary. Schultz pushed his foot down on the accelerator. Emily was pressed into the back of her seat as the car hurtled alongside the city square.

"Watch out," Lee screamed.

Schultz looked out her window. An SUV was hurtling towards them from the wrong side of a side road, clearly intent on T-boning them. Schultz moved his car over the tramline and onto the opposite side of the road. The SUV narrowly missed them.

"That was too close." Schultz looked out his rear-view mirror.

The car behind them regained control and disappeared down a side street.

"What was all that about?" Schultz asked.

"It's got to be another one of Fu's men."

"How much time have we got?"

Lee checked the timer on her phone. "Less than ten minutes."

Schultz's cell phone rang.

"That's strange," he said, looking at the screen. "Fu must've gotten bored of playing his games."

"Or he's up to something."

"Hmm." He accepted the call. "Xander, you'd better have something."

Schultz drifted around the next corner, now on the final

stretch of road to the bank.

"We have a number of locations. We're about halfway up, still working on the upper levels."

"Good. I doubt they'd have bombs in the top half. I believe he'd have them concentrated around the base and up to Andrew's office. Are there officers on the scene?"

"We have some, with more coming in."

"Bomb squad?"

"They're fifteen minutes away."

"Shit." Schultz slammed his hand on the steering wheel. "We've got ten minutes if we're going by Fu's last message."

"Can you eliminate any of the locations? Security cameras?" Emily asked.

"We'll see what we can do."

"We're only about four blocks away."

In the background, Schultz could hear Xander giving directions. He kept the phone line open.

Schultz glanced at Lee as her phone beeped. She showed him a photo.

"Holy crap. Make that eight minutes," he told Xander.

"Why? What's just happened?"

"Lee just got another photo with the timer."

"I'll see if I can run a trace on that number. It's got to be on, still."

Schultz glanced at the photo before continuing. "It definitely looks like it."

"And your number was barred before, wasn't it?"

"Yes. He's up to something, and he's got Brian with him."

"Seriously?" Xander swore lightly in the background.

"You need to put your history with him behind you and concentrate on beating them to make the building safe."

"If he has a third timer he can detonate it at any time," Emily said.

Chapter 46

Emily held the grab handle above her as Schultz yanked the handbrake and swung the car around to a complete stop, narrowly missing the police tape and a uniformed officer.

"Yep. Thanks for reminder, Lee. Greatly appreciated. Xander, hit us up with the most probable location."

"Okay." Xander paused for a second. "Coming through to your phones now."

Schultz's and Emily's phones pinged.

Clicking on the notification as she stepped out of the car, Emily said, "Okay, got it."

"One more thing, guys," Xander said. "Two cars circled the block twice before entering the carpark. Half an hour later four people in military clothing emerged from the carpark entrance and jumped in a black SUV."

"That's Fu's men. Do you have video surveillance down there?"

"No. The cameras were all sprayed with black spray paint."

"Damn. All right. Do you have the makes and models we need to look out for?"

"Just keep an eye out for black SUVs."

"Okay. Thanks, Xander."

"This way," Emily said after checking her phone. She ran towards the police tape.

"ID." An uniformed officer stepped in front of her.

"I don't have any. We're—"

"You can't enter. This is a secure area."

"You're kidding me. I'm the reason all this is happening."

"You are, are you?" The officer reached behind his back.

Emily looked around. Schultz was just catching up.

"Schultz, talk to this officer."

As he approached, Schultz pulled out his badge and held it up to the officer.

"This is Lee, Emily Lee. She's working with me on this case."

"My apologies, miss. I didn't recognize you. You're all right to go through." The officer lifted the tape up without looking at their credentials.

They stepped through and Emily began to run again.

"Down here, come on," she yelled as she ran along the side of the building and stopped a few steps into the undercover carpark.

"Shit, we're screwed," Schultz commented a few steps behind her.

"It makes sense. It's easily accessible, and you can be in and out before anyone realizes. Now, you take that side. I'll take this side." Emily began checking her side of the carpark. "Look everywhere. We've got less than six minutes."

Chapter 47

A half-empty car park was all that stood between Emily and a possible detonation beneath a modest-sized inner city multilevel building. She counted about ten vehicles parked along each side of its length, probably left behind by mid-ranking managers in the rush of evacuating the building. They consisted of a range of sedans and SUVs. Looking around, Emily noticed there weren't any cars representative of the top-end managers.

"Typical," she muttered.

"Was that black SUVs Xander saw enter here this morning?"

"Yeah, but there's four of them parked in here."

"Check everything, even if you think there couldn't be

anything hiding in there. Check, and double check."

"Yep, no worries." Emily was already approaching the first cement pillar. She scanned the area around the pillar, then up to the roof and along the wall. No sign of wires running along its length.

She walked a little quicker to the next pillar, looking all around it then along the wall. Still no signs of any explosives, wires or detonators.

The first of the cars was parked alongside the second pillar. Lying down on her stomach, she looked under the car's chassis. Nothing at the rear. She moved around to the driver's side and looked underneath, moving her phone's light up and down the length of the car.

Standing up, she quickly walked along the empty carpark spaces, keeping her eye on the roof above and the wall beside her and looking for anything abnormal, like a line of wires or a lumpy package of explosive material, or even a timer.

"Any luck?" Lee yelled out to Schultz as she approached the next car.

"No. Nothing yet," his reply came from behind her.

Looking over her shoulder, she saw he was only a quarter of his way into the carpark, moving on from the first of the parked black SUVs. He'd always been too cautious, always scrutinizing everything before he was happy enough to move on. Nothing had changed in all the years she'd known him.

Turning around, she walked around the next car, looking it over. It was a common six-cylinder sedan with an enlarged exhaust and standard sports body kit. The make and model weren't one she'd expected to see parked amongst the other cars there.

She looked along the wall in front of the parked car and above. Nothing except for a few pipes running along the wall. Carefully lying down on her stomach, she moved her phone's light up and down.

Oh! She paused the light on the rear of the car.

"Schultz."

"Found something?"

"Yeah, possibly." Emily moved around to the rear of the car.

Behind her, she heard Schultz's heavy footsteps approaching.

"What've you got?"

Emily looked over her shoulder and saw Schultz crouching down, trying to peer under the car.

"You'll need to get down a bit lower than that."

Watching Schultz gingerly lowering his body to the cement floor, she chuckled.

"Yes, very funny."

"Right there." Emily moved her phone to highlight a flashing light.

Schultz rolled onto his back and wiggled underneath the rear of the car.

"Keep the light steady."

The seconds ticked by slowly as Emily held the light in position.

"What is it?" she asked, trying to peer underneath.

Schultz began wiggling out and Emily moved back.

"Decoy." He held up a small rectangular box with a flashing light.

"You sure?"

"Certain. There's no wires leading anywhere."

"Bastard." Emily placed one hand on her hip and rubbed her forehead with her other hand.

"Let's keep moving. It's got to be in here somewhere."

Looking deep into the carpark her sight fell on two reverse-parked SUVs, one on each side of the carpark. Her stomach began to churn.

"Schultz, those have to be the cars." She pointed towards them.

"Maybe they are. But continue checking everything up to them."

Emily took a few steps towards the vehicles.

"Lee," Schultz yelled.

Pulling her eyes away from the parked SUVs, she continued looking along the wall and roof, picking up her pace, jogging along the empty spaces where she was confident there was nothing suspicious. Just empty walls and piping run along the roof.

The two parked SUVs were now only five car park spaces away and their time was nearly gone. Inching closer to the cars, Emily felt the violent twists and churning in her stomach increasing.

Her phone vibrated in her back pocket.

"Schultz, less than four minutes."

There was no reply.

"Schultz." She turned around. His legs were poking out from beneath the second black SUV on his side of the car park, his bare ankles exposed.

Shaking her head, Emily quickly ran towards the black SUV, the last car parked on her side. Looking between the two cars she noticed they had sequential number plates.

"Schultz, sequential number plates," she yelled over her shoulder.

"What are the odds of that? I'll be there in a minute."

"We don't have a minute."

There were two empty spaces between the SUVs and the end of the carpark, right before an emergency exit with the door partially open.

The roof was clear. Emily moved towards the wall and stopped. A set of wires were leading from a hole in the roof line, right in the corner, down the wall. She followed the wires along the wall; they turned and continued along the cement floor until they got to the car.

Emily crouched down onto all fours and flashed her light under the chassis. Her phone's light illuminated the place where the spare wheel well would usually be.

Rolling onto her back, she wriggled underneath the car.

"Oh, hell." Angling her head towards the other side of the carpark, she yelled out, "Schultz. I definitely have a problem."

Chapter 48

"I'll check the other one," Schultz yelled as he ran up.

"Yep, quick. We don't have long." Emily stared at the red illuminated numbers above her. "We've got less than three minutes."

"Plenty of time."

"I don't think so," she muttered as she shook her head, her eyes on the timer. A cell phone and a series of colored wires linked the timer to a bundle of unidentifiable explosives.

"When was the last time you detonated a device?" Emily angled her head towards Schultz.

"Last week, and it was a piece of cake."

"Right, and you're going to tell me you've got wire cutters in your back pocket, too?"

"Sure do. As instructed, always prepared."

"Seriously?"

There was no answer. She turned her head towards the other parked SUV and saw Schultz lying underneath.

"What've you got there?" she asked.

"This one appears to be all clear from the outside." He scrambled out from underneath the car and stopped next to it. "I can't see anything inside, not with this dark illegal window tint."

"Well, I can see this one very clearly. Can you get here like, NOW? Before we blow up, preferably." She turned back towards the underside of her car.

Gingerly holding the colored wires in her hand, she used her other hand to lightly tug the first wire.

"What are you doing?" Schultz asked.

Emily's hands jolted a little. "Don't do that to me again!"

"Do you know what you're doing there?" Schultz wriggled on his back until he was alongside Emily.

"Not really, but I have found this loose wire." She held one of the wires in her hand.

"You sure it was already unattached?"

"Yes. Which one do we need to cut?"

"Shimmy over a little and I'll have a good look."

Emily shuffled over and Schultz moved in.

"Light?" he asked.

"Shit." She grabbed her hand.

"What happened?" Schultz asked, concerned.

"It's all right. Just a cramp in my fingers. Pinched nerve, I think."

"You still having troubles with that?"

"Let's not go there."

Emily activated the light with her good hand and shone it towards the timer.

"Good. Okay, what have we got here?" he asked to no one in particular.

Emily looked at the timer. It ticked down to double digits. "Less than a minute."

"Shh, really don't need to hear that."

"You can see it, too."

"Lee." He turned towards her, his eyes narrowed.

"Just saying." She shrugged her shoulders.

Schultz pressed a button behind his ear. "Xander?"

Silence. "I've got you," Xander replied.

"I'm sending you a photo." Schultz took a photo of the bomb and sent it through. "We need to know how to deactivate it."

"Okay." Xander paused, "Okay. I've got it. Holy mother. This is going to take some hunting."

"You have 30 seconds," Emily ground out through gritted teeth.

"Shine your light there." Schultz pointed towards the rear of the car.

Emily shifted the light until the beam fell on the set of wires running along the chassis.

"Where do those wires go?"

"Along the floor and up the wall into the roof."

"Into the roof?"

"Yes, freshly drilled."

"Holy…" His voice trailed off before he continued. "There's got to be more explosives in this building than just this one."

"If we can defuse this one, will it stop the others?"

"Hoping so, but we'll know shortly. Do the wires run anywhere else?"

"Why? What's wrong?"

"There's a set of wires running into the car." He looked up and down the length of the SUV before continuing. "Into the trunk. These ones here." Schultz placed a finger on a set of wires and Emily shifted the beam of light.

"I'll go check." Emily began to wriggle away.

"We don't have time." He pointed to the timer. It showed 20 seconds. "You should get outta here."

"I'm not leaving. We're going to do this together. Do you think Xander will find something in time?"

"I highly doubt it. Time for plan B." Schultz pulled a pair of wire cutters from his rear pants pocket.

"You were serious!" Emily shook her head, chuckling to herself. "Unbelievable."

Schultz's phone vibrated. Pressing the device behind his ear, he answered, "Xander. That was quick. Tell me you have something for us."

"Yes and no. This bomb was a direct hit from the gangs straight from Asia. We've just never seen one on our home turf yet. We don't have any procedures on deactivating anything remotely like this."

"How do we stop it?" Schultz snapped.

"We can't. I mean... No one on our home soil has been able to successfully stop one yet."

"What do you mean, no one?"

"Well, it hasn't been attempted."

"How far out is the squad?"

"Five minutes."

"That's five minutes too long. We're going to have to do this old school. Xander, if I don't get through this... It's been nice working with you. Take good care."

Schultz disconnected the call.

"You've done this before, haven't you?" Lee looked between the bomb and Schultz.

"Only in training. Nothing like this."

"Comforting."

"You can always leave."

"Not enough time." Lee looked at the timer on her phone. "Ten seconds."

"Okay, think. Which wires?" he whispered.

Lee looked on, keeping her light focused on the wires. "The red and black ones. To the side, there."

"Why not the ones on this side?" Schultz moved the pliers to the opposite end.

"They're Fu's favorite colors. He does everything in red and black. When I was growing up, he used to give me and my sister electronic circuits to disarm. Every time, it was the same two wires, red and black."

Schultz moved the pliers to where she was pointing.

"Please be right." He closed his eyes and cut into the wires. Nothing happened.

He peered one open. The green light was still lit.

"Shit." He punched the cement flooring.

"I honestly-"

"Hang on a minute."

Schultz placed his hand around the cell phone and wiggled it a little. There was some movement. He pulled a little more and it came free.

Emily grabbed the phone from Schultz, rolled out from under the car and shot two bullets through the screen.

"Lights turned red," Schultz advised.

Looking at the smoking phone, she replied, "I think you might have done it."

A rumble sounded nearby. Emily turned towards the sound. Dust sifted through the ceiling and lingered in the air for a moment before settling onto the floor.

"I thought you checked up there." Schultz turned to Emily.

"No time. I only got this far." She pointed to the black SUV.

"Stay here." Schultz pointed his finger towards a spot between them.

"Yeah, not going to happen," she muttered as he was halfway to the emergency exit door.

Walking around the vehicle, Emily felt for the trunk release. She pressed the button. Nothing. She tried it again. Still nothing. Taking aim, she fired a couple of shots into the lock.

"What was that?"

She peered around the rear of the car. Schultz was now standing by the emergency exit door.

"Trunk wouldn't open."

He shook his head and turned back to inspect the bulging door. Carefully feeling around the edge of the door and the exposed door frame, Schultz checked for wires. Content there weren't any, he edged the door open.

And took a step back.

It sat there, in the center of the platform.

Waiting.

Another one. Only part of it had managed to explode. Looking over the contraption from where they stood, they couldn't find any obvious triggering devices or LED lights.

What they did find were three tubes of bubbling liquid, full almost to the top.

Schultz carefully closed the door, grabbed Lee by the arm and sprinted towards the street.

"What's going on?" Her legs were struggling to keep up.

"We're getting out of here. Now."

"I found... another one... in the trunk," Emily said, gasping for breath. "Glass cylinders, bubbly liquid inside, just like the ones behind the exit door."

"Great."

The blinding sunlight of the setting sun blinded them as they ran clear of the carpark.

"Move. Get out." They both waved their hands in the air.

"There's two bombs about to go off." Emily pulled an

officer by his arm, running as fast as she could despite her dwindling stamina.

Ahead of them, the onlookers were now running either up or down the street opposite the building.

Sheltered behind the street corner opposite, her breathing rapid and shallow, Emily bent over to try and catch her breath.

"Will one of you tell me what on earth is going on here before I charge both of you?" The officer she'd dragged behind them looked first at Emily then Schultz.

Schultz, bent over, held up his badge.

"So sorry. I didn't recognize you, Schultz. You must be Lee. You've had an eventful day." He shook her hand.

Lee waved her hand, brushing the compliment off.

"What's going on in there?" the officer asked.

In between shallow breaths, Schultz did his best to relay the situation. "There's two black SUVs parked opposite each other, sequential number plates. One has the trunk popped open, the lock shot."

The officer raised an eyebrow and looked between them both.

"I'll explain later. The original bomb under the chassis has been defused. Lee, you got it?"

Emily handed over the beaten-up phone to the officer.

"That's what we pulled from the one underneath the chassis."

"There's another one in the trunk of the same car," Emily interrupted. "Clear cylinders with bubbly liquid inside."

"How many cylinders?" the officer asked, his notepad and

pen ready.

"Four."

"Xander has relayed us a copy of the device, the one this was attached to." The officer waved the phone. "But there was no mention of cylinders."

"We've only just discovered them, literally moments before we ran out of there." Emily waved her hand back towards the undercover carpark.

"At the far end of the carpark," Schultz continued with his debrief. "There was a small explosion, not long after our timer clocked down to zero. It's knocked a bulge in the emergency exit door, but it hasn't fully exploded, and dust came down from all along the ceiling."

The officer depressed the button on his handheld radio. "Okay, boys."

"You're our bomb squad." Lee raised her eyebrow towards the officer.

"Time to suit up and send the AI in. We've got volatile liquids in there and a possible partially detonated device."

Chapter 49

Emily sat side-on in one of the nearby patrol cars, her feet over the edge, resting on the asphalt, a blanket wrapped around her. Pulling the corner of the blanket up, she bit its edge as she watched one of the suited bomb squad team members guide a robotic device towards the entrance of the undercover carpark.

It wasn't long until the robot disappeared, enveloped by the darkness. Emily lent back into the seat and closed her eyes.

Her father sat in front of her.

"Dad," she screamed out but he didn't respond.

Looking around, she noticed they were back in the warehouse.

Opposite her, her father was still shackled to the chair,

slowly gaining consciousness. Uncle Fu stood behind him, the gun pressed against the back of her father's head. She saw his mouth moving but couldn't hear what he was saying.

Emily tried to run towards her father but her feet wouldn't move; it was like they were shackled to the floor. Her father looked in her direction, his eyes pleading. "I'm sorry," she read on his lips before his head slumped forward. A trail of blood traversed around his neck and down under his shirt.

Screaming, her arms outstretched towards her father, Emily fought to move closer to him as warm tears rolled down her cheeks.

"Lee. Lee." In the distance, she thought she heard her name being called.

"Lee, wake up," the voice came again, this time a little louder.

She felt her body shaking, slipping backwards.

"Lee."

Her father faded in the distance. Crying, her hands waving wildly, Emily opened her eyes.

"What? What's wrong?" She looked around, bewildered, unable to merge her dream with reality.

"Looked like you were having a nightmare." Schultz placed his hand on her knee. "I should get you home. Get some rest."

"Home? What's that?"

"Fair call. My place then. You need some rest."

"No. No." Lee sat up. "I'm all good. I just closed my eyes for a second. I'll be all right. Any news from in there?" She nodded towards the carpark.

"Nothing yet. They're keeping tight-lipped."

"Hmm. Okay. No explosion yet, then?"

"Dead quiet on that front."

"I need to make a quick phone call."

She received a strange look from Schultz but he didn't question her as she stood up.

Keeping the blanket wrapped around her, she walked away from the car towards the opposite street corner, tapping a number into her cell phone. She'd just finished crossing the street when her call was answered.

"Hello?" a weary male's voice answered.

"Harry?" Lee looked towards Schultz and the congregating officers. Everyone had their attention on the carpark entrance. Schultz turned around and smiled at her. She returned the smile and gave him a thumbs-up, letting him know she was all good.

"Yeah. Emily, is that you?"

"Yes, it is. I need you to hold tight for a little bit longer. Can you do that?"

"I thought you were killed in that explosion out along the foreshore, near some marina."

"Explosion?"

"Yeah. I got a video message. Would've been less than five minutes ago."

Emily could hear Sharon agreeing in the background.

"Did the message come through with a set of numbers, like a cell phone number?"

"Hang on a moment, I'll check."

She could hear him tapping and cursing as he navigated his phone.

"Okay. You still there?" Harry returned to Emily.

"Yes, I am."

"Good. It does look like a cell phone number."

"Great. Can you read the numbers to me?" Emily activated her phone speakers and pulled up her contact list.

Harry began to read out the numbers and Emily typed them into her phone. The automated search scrolled through her list of contacts, narrowing the list as she typed in each number.

Harry read out the last digit and only one name remained on her list.

"Fu," Emily whispered.

"Who's that?"

"No one." Lee took the call off her phone's speakers before continuing. "Can you please send the video through to this number?"

"All right. But it doesn't sound like no one to me. You sure you're telling me the whole story?"

"Yes, I am." Emily rubbed her forehead. "I just like knowing everyone who alleges I'm dead. Did the message say anything else?"

Emily could hear scrambling before Harry returned to the call. "It reads, 'Tick tock. One problem down. You're next.'"

"Can you please forward that to me, too?"

"You're not telling me everything. Who is this Fu guy? He is a guy, right?"

"I don't know him. I've only heard of him."

"Then why do you know his cell phone number? You really aren't good at this game. You think I'm stupid or something? How would you like to hear a murder?"

"I'm sorry. No, you're not stupid. I've had a long day and I'm just exhausted. Fu is someone I'm investigating. I kept a record of his contact number."

"Is this guy responsible for stealing my property?"

Emily closed her eyes and took a deep breath before replying. "It looks that way."

"And you have all his contact information? You know where he lives?"

"I don't have his address; that one has been withheld from public record."

"Hmm. Sounds like a shady guy to me."

"Yes, he is. Have you been able to send the message through to me?"

"You should..." He paused. She heard him tapping away at his phone. "You should get it in a moment. Any movement on getting my farm back?"

"It's with the right people. After this is all over, I'm hoping you'll be all set to get it back."

"You're hoping?"

Emily heard a metallic click followed by a shriek from Sharon.

"Hold up, hold up. I'm pulling everything I can to get it back to you. These things take time."

"Time that we apparently don't have, according to that

video."

"How do you know that? The message doesn't say anything about time."

"You don't need to be Einstein to work that one out. Tick tock, the clock's ticking. By the sounds of it, you don't have much time."

Emily paused, dumbfounded. He might be a farmer but there were no flies on him. A hard worker, supporting his country, and having his livelihood snatched from underneath him.

"Please," Emily continued. "Please put that gun down and listen to me."

There was silence, then a rustle.

"Sharon, can you hear me?" Emily yelled into her phone.

"Y-yes," Sharon's voice wavered in the background. "Yes, I can... hear you."

"Are you safe?"

"Yes." Her voice was now closer to the phone. "He's collapsed on the floor."

"Okay. Can you please take me off the speaker phone?"

"Done."

"Is Harry okay?" Emily asked.

"He was a little shaky and on edge before."

"Do you know if he has any medical conditions?"

"No, not that I'm aware of."

"Kick his gun away and then I need you to see if he has a pulse."

"You want me to... to touch this gun-yielding maniac?"

"Sharon, he's far from a maniac. He's just a desperate man wanting what's best for him and his family."

"This was so not in my job description."

"Sharon. Listen to me. This will be all over soon."

"Not soon enough." She paused before continuing, "He's got a pulse."

"Good. I need you to roll him on to his side."

"Seriously?"

"Sharon. Roll him onto his side." Emily's voice was firm.

Schultz looked over, his eyes narrowed, his hands gesturing to her, wanting to know what was going on. Smiling, she gave him another thumbs-up.

"Done. Andrew had better be giving me a pay rise after today."

"That's the least of your worries."

"What do you mean?"

"Listen to me very carefully and don't say or do anything. Understand?"

"Mmmhmm," she replied.

"This is for your ears only: The building is hot."

"Hot? What do you mean?"

Emily turned away from everyone, taking a few steps away from the growing crowd of onlookers. Lowering her voice, she replied, "We've got one disarmed. The squad are in the carpark right now, ensuring the others are made safe."

Sharon gasped. She could hear Harry stir in the background.

"You'll be safe there. When I'm given the all-clear, I'll

personally come up there and bring you both down. Okay?"

"Yes."

"Good. Now I need to leave you. If Harry awakes before I get there, please let him now I'll be up shortly. I'm just getting some wounds dressed. Okay?"

"Emily, please be safe."

Chapter 50

Harry, still shaking, tried to focus on his watch.

"How long was I out for?"

"Not long. You get them often?"

Harry looked around and noticed the gun lying on the floor just out of reach. Staggering onto all fours he crawled over and picked up the gun then used the nearby wall to support himself as he stood up.

Turning around, he aimed the gun at Sharon, his hand shaking. "That woman had better have some news soon, for your sake."

Sharon's lower lip was quivering. She slowly moved her head up then down.

"Sorry, sweetheart. Your boss has crossed the line too many

times. He needs to learn the hard way. And you crossed the line too when you tried to remove this from me."

Something fell off the desk and smashed onto the floor. Harry stopped and stared at the broken shards of china then at Sharon. She shook her head.

The computer screen began to jump across the desk. Harry spun around. A painting fell onto the floor.

"Earthquake!" Sharon screamed.

Harry peered out the window and looked around and down. There wasn't any commotion out on the street. "It's not an earthquake."

"Then what the hell is it?"

She stood up, ready to take cover, her chair banging against a filing cabinet. Harry swung around, his gun pointed straight at her.

"Sit back down. Don't move if you value your life." He walked towards the office door, his gun pointed at Sharon.

Harry peered out of the office and down the corridor and felt his eyes widen.

What on Earth happened here? he thought.

He put one foot outside the office, making sure he kept the other foot inside the doorway. The floor and all furnishings had dropped at least half a foot, some a bit more. They were all tilted by small angles. Not like they'd been thrown about. No. An angle like... the floor was on a slant. Like something had given way underneath, beneath one corner.

His phone vibrated against his leg. Staring at the

devastation before him, Harry fumbled through his pocket until he found it.

1 new message, the screen read.

He tapped the screen and a video began to play.

The video showed an Asian man sitting in a small room. Along one side, it looked like water was moving around him, in small wave-like motions.

"Well, well, well. If you're watching this you haven't been arrested yet." The Asian man chuckled. "It is of no concern to you who I am. All I'm going to say is you've stirred the pot today. Brought unwanted attention to my company."

The camera was adjusted to show some beefy men in the background who stood shoulder to shoulder. There was barely any room between the ceiling and the top of their heads. Water also lapped at the windows beside them.

"That first shake was just a taste of what's to come," he continued. "Stand down from your... immature protest, and there'll be no more. If you continue your shenanigans... there'll be more of them, bigger ones. Your safety... No, your life, your survival cannot be guaranteed." He winked and the video stopped.

"A bomb?" Harry muttered. "What the hell?" He turned to Sharon. "Who are these people? Was that Fu?"

She shrugged her shoulders.

Shaking his head, Harry stepped out of the office as he dialed a number. The line rang through his phone's speakers.

"Hello?" a softly spoken woman answered.

"Victoria?" he checked his phone to ensure he'd dialed the

right number.

"Harry? Is that you?"

"Yes, it is. You sound exhausted."

"Are you okay? I've seen the news about the bank. You were going there today, weren't you? You haven't done anything stupid, have you?"

Harry swallowed and closed his eyes. His stomach twisted and turned as he replied, "No, I was in and out this morning."

He could hear his wife breathe a deep sigh of relief.

"What did the bank manager have to say?"

"I'll... I'll talk to you tonight."

"Okay. Hope we get our home back. The kids are fighting each other over the smallest of things. Not sure how much longer we can stand being cooped up in this room."

He pictured the chaos she was dealing with, that they were all dealing with.

"The wheels are in motion."

"Oh, good. That's great to hear."

Harry thought carefully about his next words. He looked over his shoulder. Sharon quickly turned her head away. Stepping into the corridor, he pulled the door until it was almost shut.

"I'll be home soon. Just not sure when."

"What's wrong?" Victoria's voice trembled. "What aren't you telling me?"

"Please give the children a hug and tell them I love them all very much."

"You're scaring me. What's going on?"

"I love you."

He disconnected the call and walked back into the office. His fingers were trembling as he pocketed his phone.

"What's happened?" Sharon asked.

"Nothing. Must've been an earth tremor."

"Right." Sharon raised an eyebrow. "Is that the story you're going to stick with?"

Harry didn't reply.

"If you're going to lie, at least make an effort to sound convincing."

"Tell me a little more about these investors." Harry pulled a chair alongside Sharon and sat down.

"You want me to cooperate with you now? You want my help?"

"Yes, please. We're in trouble."

Sharon shook her head looking bewildered but spoke after a moment. "The investors are actually an organization, if you can call them that, and you don't want to get on the wrong side of them. I guess, by that video you've just received, that they're the ones behind that 'tremor'."

"Continue." Harry maintained his poker face.

"They exploit personnel in the finance industry who are vulnerable and have the most to lose. Anything to get their way."

"Like leaking your boss' affair to his wife and family?"

Sharon lowered her head and quietly replied, "Yes."

"What connection does Emily Lee have to all this? Looking at the file notes, I couldn't see how she was connected to any of it."

"She's... she's been getting close to unravelling the land transfers between Andrew and the corporation."

"There's more to it. Why is this boss guy so hell-bent on destroying her?"

"Yes, there is more, but it's not my place to say."

Harry stood over her and pressed his gun barrel against the back of her head. "It's not your place to say? Who gave you the authority to decide what you will and will not say? Tell me now. What is Emily's connection to all of this?"

Sharon closed her eyes and composed herself before replying. "The man you've been talking to today?"

"Yeah. Little grumpy ole' Chinese man?"

"That is Emily's uncle."

"Shit. Is she in on this scam, too? Wanting a cut from her uncle's cake?"

"No. Quite the opposite. I overheard a conversation between Fu-"

"The grumpy Chinese man?"

"Yeah, him, and Andrew a few days ago. I overheard Andrew telling Fu about Emily's recent visit. Well, Fu cut loose. Banishing her from the family, and some gibberish about her not even being blood."

"So, how serious is this Fu guy with his threats?"

"Very. Very much so. Nothing gets in his way. He gets what he wants, when he wants it."

"Well, we're in a lot of shit, then. Hopefully Emily can get my farm back before this place collapses."

"What do you mean?"

"That wasn't a small earth tremor, it was a small bomb, and apparently there's more lined up for us, bigger ones."

"We need to get out of here."

"We're not going anywhere. The minute we step outside we're done for. The police are there, waiting. I'll either be shot on sight or arrested. Then where will my family be? All this will have been for nothing. No doubt there'll be camera crews down there lying in wait. No, I don't need that. Hell, my family have no need to see that."

"That's not true. I'll vouch for you when we get out of here."

"That's nice. But Emily is doing her thing. I trust that. We just need to wait and hope she comes through with the goods."

"And if she doesn't?"

"Hopefully what you sent her will be enough to set the record straight after we're gone."

Chapter 51

The motion from the waves rocked Fu from side to side as he navigated the steel rod steps. He nodded to a suited man who assisted him up the last step from their pod and onto the boat.

Placing his cell phone back against his ear, he continued his call. "It's time to wake up the mother."

"I... I don't mean to question you. But... Are you sure? Aren't we better off disappearing?" a man with a deep Eastern European accent asked.

"You are correct. You shouldn't be questioning me. You get remunerated for doing as you're told. You're not paid to think. I do the thinking."

"There's police swarming all over the building."

"Not my problem. You need to get in there somehow and

set them off. If you pull this off, successfully, it will be the mother payload for you. You can take a few months off and soak up some sun with some islander ladies."

"Sounds good, boss. If I get out of there alive."

"That will be up to you."

Fu hung up the phone.

"That city isn't going to know what's hit it. Emily and her cop boyfriend will be gone. Forever."

Everyone chuckled and patted him on the back.

"I trust you've been keeping everyone on board occupied?"

The suited man nodded, his face blank.

Fu returned his attention to his men. "Time to celebrate, boys." He snapped his fingers at the suited man. "Bring out the drinks and the ladies."

Chapter 52

Emily looked at her watch for the tenth time in the last few minutes. The seconds barely ticked by as she waited for the devices to be defused.

"Keeping an eye on the time isn't going to speed it up," Schultz said as he leant against the patrol car.

"Do they usually take this long?"

"No. Longer."

Emily groaned.

Schultz laughed. I'd hate to be on a stake-out with you. We haven't been waiting that long, and you're already itchy to get moving. There'll be plenty of time to get your mate down."

"Excuse me," a male's voice came from a distance.

Emily heard it but ignored him.

"Miss. Excuse me, miss."

Emily turned around. A lean man barely in his mid-twenties was waving as he made his way towards them.

"Look at this crazy." Schultz turned to Emily.

"How did he get through the police barricades?"

"Not sure." Schultz stepped in front of her.

The man called out again, this time louder, "Miss. Sir. Excuse me."

Emily leant out of the car to peer around Schultz. Two police officers were holding the man back.

"I have some important news regarding the bomb at the bank."

"What bomb?" She dropped her blanket and took a few steps towards him, her arms crossed over her body, stopping a little more than an arm's reach from him.

"I tried telling the officer here," he nodded his head to the officer on his right, "that I saw parts of the building crumble away."

"What do you mean, crumble away?"

"There was a rumble. Some of the upper windows shook. Some of the rendering broke off."

Emily stared at him. The young man with his boyish looks stared back at her. He didn't flinch.

"Where about did you see the rubble falling from?" Schultz asked.

They turned towards the building. Emily couldn't see anything that looked out of place.

"Up about... two, three," he pointed to each window as he

counted the levels, "four, five. About six windows up on the far-left side. There's a bit missing around the window."

"I don't see anything wrong. Are you wasting an officer's time?" Schultz asked, rubbing his neck as he looked back at the young man.

"No, no, officer. I wouldn't do that."

"Detective." He raised his eyebrow. "Thank you."

"Schultz, I think he's right."

"You must have better eyesight than me."

"Front tower, second window from the left side. Top right corner. Do you see it?"

"Only just. I think. Can't be too certain."

Emily scanned the immediate area around the damaged window before moving up the street a little farther, trying to get a better angle from around the corner.

"Schultz," she whispered. "We have a problem."

The nearby officers turned at the sound of her voice but she pulled Schultz closer and turned around so they wouldn't be overheard.

"There's more than just that one damaged window. There's a few of them. Next level down, two windows have plaster missing. And that's what we can see from here. If that corner has damage, I'd be expecting to see some damage around the side as well."

"There's only one thing that can cause that." Schultz placed his hand above his eyes and blocked out some of the glare from the sun.

"Those two bombs are only the beginning. I need to get a

better look around the other side."

"Hold up a moment."

Emily followed the direction he was looking. Officers stirred around the carpark entrance. He walked towards them.

"Thank you for your information." Emily smiled at the stranger. "Please leave your details with the officers here and we'll be in touch if we need any further information from you."

"Glad I could be of assistance." He extended his open hand over the officers' shoulders.

Calloused and dirty knuckles greeted her.

"It's okay, officers."

They stepped aside just enough for his arm to lower to a comfortable level.

Trying not to grimace, she exchanged handshakes. His grip was surprisingly strong. The exchange continued for much longer than she would usually accept, so Emily pulled her arm back but he held her hand firm. An evil grin emerged on his face. Emily tried again to pull her hand away, and this time he allowed her hand to slide out of his grip. Small particles of dirt rubbed against her hand as she drew it away.

Forcing a smile, she turned around and hurried towards Schultz.

"Schultz," she said as she stepped into line next to him. "Please tell me you have someone from forensics here."

"Why?" He turned to see her arm extended. "He was that bad, was he?"

"I felt something grimy rub against my hand as I tried to

pull away." She looked over his shoulder but he had disappeared. "Something doesn't feel right about him."

"He's probably a worker from one of the skyscraper projects."

Emily raised her eyebrow at him. "Did he look like a construction worker? Those were expensive shoes he was wearing."

"I don't know." Schultz shrugged.

"I want my hand swabbed, and whatever else they do. Then I'm going to check the other corner of the building. If there's damage we're in trouble."

"I'll come with you."

"No, I'll be all right. You're probably needed here."

"I wasn't giving you an option."

Schultz flagged down a nearby forensics officer and he took evidence from her hand and sleeve.

"I'll need your shirt," the forensics specialist said as he took the last swab from Emily's shirt.

"My shirt?"

"It's evidence. Along with these." He placed the now enveloped swab with the others.

"No. You can cut off what you need. But my shirt is staying on my back."

"Why are you being difficult? I'm doing you a favor by doing these swabs here. What makes you think it's all related to what's happening here?"

"He had cement particles on his top."

"That could be from anywhere."

"Cement dust particles."

"If we do find anything on your shirt, the evidence cannot be used in court."

"Yep. Whatever."

Emily looked up at the building, searching for any other damaged windows, when everyone around her began clapping.

One of the bomb squad members emerged from the carpark, leaning back as he carried a heavy metal box out. The officers kept their distance.

Stopping in the middle of the road, he placed the box down and removed his helmet.

"Clear. Other one will be out in a minute."

"Excuse me." Emily walked over to him. "Could they have caused any damage six floors up?"

He gave her an uncertain look. "No. The one that partly detonated, if it had fully exploded, would probably have only caused minor damage in the stairwell. Not enough to be felt six floors up."

"Hmmm. Okay. And the bubbly liquid?"

"Colored water."

"Okay, thank you."

"Why do you ask?"

"I just want to check something out first. Don't go too far."

His mouth fell open as Emily walked towards the corner. She could hear Schultz's racing steps not far behind her.

Shielding her eyes from the sun's glare bouncing off the windows, she looked up to the fifth and sixth level windows.

"Holy mother of—" Schultz said.

"Who knows how many more are in that tower?" Emily shook her head.

The devastation was obvious here. Sheets of plaster between the windows had split and fallen off. Steel frames were now visible. Windows had cracked.

Emily ran to the officer manning the barrier.

"How long have you been manning this boundary for?"

"All day. What's the problem?"

"You didn't feel or hear anything?"

The officer shook his head.

"You sure?" Her eyes narrowed as she stared at him.

"Are you doubting me?"

"Just asking. Strange that someone who is patrolling the line didn't see or hear that rubble fall down." She pointed up towards level six.

He glanced up for a second before returning his attention to Emily.

"I can't help you. Sorry." He turned around and spoke into his handheld radio as he walked towards his car.

"He's hiding something," Emily murmured.

"What, him?" Schultz replied. "Don't think so. He's one of our best officers."

"Hmmm." Emily pulled out her phone.

She dialed a recent number on her call list. The line rang twice before it was answered.

"You got an answer," Harry answered.

"We're working on it."

"Time's ticking. You don't have long before I blow her

brains out."

Sharon shrieked in the background. Emily could only imagine he'd placed the barrel of the gun against her head.

"I have a question. Have you experienced any tremors today?"

"Besides the one you were meant to have been in?"

"Yes," Emily replied, getting frustrated.

"A small one." He paused before continuing. "Nothing major. Probably an earthquake."

"More than an earthquake," she heard Sharon yell out in the background.

"What did she say?" Emily asked.

"Nothing. We did feel a tremor. We're all good."

"Okay, thank you. I'll have some news for you shortly."

She disconnected the phone call.

"Schultz, you got a spare handheld?" She eyed his radio.

"In the car. Why?"

"Good. I'll grab it on the way past. We need to sweep each level. There's more than those two devices. Can you organize that?"

Schultz didn't argue, not this time. This was the only time she didn't want to be right. She was hoping to be proven wrong, for the sake of everyone's safety.

"And I'll get Harry and Sharon out safely."

She glanced over her shoulder. The officer she was suspicious of was on his phone. As soon as he saw Emily looking at him he turned his back to her. She followed the direction he was looking. Nearby, the young man who had advised them of the explosion was also on his phone and appeared to be looking directly at the officer.

Emily's stomach began to churn. Something was fishy, alright.

Chapter 53

Emily stepped out of the emergency stairwell and onto the sixth level floor. Stopping in the doorway, she felt her mouth drop open as she took in the devastation before her.

Cracked and partially fallen plaster sheets revealed the building's skeleton. Office furnishings leant towards the rear of the building.

A piece of plaster freed itself from the last few strands that was holding it to the wall and, landing on the floor with a thud, sent a flurry of dust into the air.

Wind whistled in through the new hole in the wall, the building next door now visible. Dust and papers flew around the office space.

Looking a little farther along, towards the area where the

floor was sinking, Emily noticed that another piece of plaster wasn't far from falling off the wall.

The floor shook. Office furniture grated along the floor, sliding towards the rear of the building. Looking up the wide passage, all Emily saw were closed office doors. Towards the far end, the floor was beginning to slant backwards.

"Where are you, guys?" She scrunched her hair in her hand as she looked around.

Running to the first door, she pulled down on the handle. It didn't move.

Banging on the door with her fists, she yelled out, "Harry. You there?"

With more force behind her punches, she banged on the door again. Silence.

Running to the next door on the opposite side of the hallway, she tried the handle. It was also locked.

"Where is he?" she asked herself as she looked around.

All the doors were shut, and all blinds were drawn.

"Are they even still here?"

She tried the next two doors, which were also locked.

The floor rumbled again. The furniture at the end of the passage slid and shifted further. Another sheet of plaster fell off the wall.

"Level one cleared," Schultz reported over her handheld radio.

"Top level cleared," another male's voice reported.

Emily was now halfway down the passage and was running out of doors fast.

Stopping outside the second to last door, she held the door handle and pressed her ear against the door. She could hear a muffled male's voice murmuring something.

Clenching her jaw, she pushed down on the door handle, expecting it to stop moving at any moment. But her hand kept moving downwards. Her heart pounded faster. The snib clicked and the door creaked open.

The murmuring stopped.

Emily reached for her gun but didn't find it. *Fu,* she thought, remembering he'd taken it from her in the warehouse.

Unarmed, she slowly pushed the door open.

"Harry. It's over." Emily took a step towards him.

He turned and pointed his gun at her chest.

She raised her arms in front of her. "I'm not armed. Look." She turned around, her back towards him. "See, you've got the only gun."

Sharon shrieked and Emily swung around. Harry had his gun pressed to his own temple.

"You don't want to do this," she said as she lowered her arms. "What will your wife and family think? How will your children live if they found out their father killed himself?"

"What difference does it make? No matter how you look at it, I'm a dead man." Harry pressed his gun further into the side of his head.

"We're so close. This is nearly over. Do you really want to do this?" Emily looked at Sharon then back to Harry. "Do you want some good news? It looks like the information you and

Sharon forwarded me is going to open a whole can of worms. What Andrew did to you and your family, to your friends and neighbors... That information is all out there now. The waves are growing into a full-blown tsunami."

Harry loosened his grip on the gun.

"What good is any of that when the farm isn't back in my name?"

"And you're right, it's not. Not yet. These things take a little time. They've got to follow the paper trail and get it all retracted. You know legal departments and their red tape."

"We don't have time."

"What do you mean? There's still plenty of time. You've got a lot of years ahead of you yet. There's still a lot of fight in you."

"Show her." Harry lowered his gun until it was aimed towards Sharon.

Emily took a step towards Harry, her eyes on the gun. She stopped in her tracks when she saw him nudge Sharon's shoulder with the gun barrel, pushing her towards her computer.

Sharon paused for a second and then opened the email attachment. A video played.

Fu appeared on the screen, sitting at a table, with port holes behind him. Emily assumed he was in a boat cabin.

"My cherished Emily, if you're watching this, I take it you've met Harry and Andrew's mistress, Sharon." Fu's head moved to the side as he thought out loud, "Oh, isn't his wife going to be ecstatic when she learns of his extra-curricular activities? Anyhow, back to you, my dearest Emily." He returned his attention to the camera. "Do you really think you're smarter than me? Ah, don't answer. I already know your response. You're sitting there gritting your teeth. Biting your tongue."

Emily unclenched her jaw but her eyes were still narrowed as the video continued to play.

"You escaped the first bomb. Well done. I would've been disappointed if you hadn't. Can't say some of your cop friends were as fortunate. Anyhow, by the time this is played, no doubt you will be sweeping all the levels of that building. Do you think you'll find anything before time runs out? Yes, that's right, you have until quarter past to find them all." He paused and stared at the camera before continuing, "Let me ask you this. Is the human risk worth it? How many uniforms are you willing to lose so two people can live?" Fu leant back in his chair and stared right at Emily.

With his head resting against his hand, he continued, "You don't go into battle with me and come out in front. No one does. Good luck, and I wish you well." Fu turned around.

The video stopped with his back to them.

"Shit, that little prick. When did this video come through?" She looked between Harry and Sharon. "How long do we have left?"

"It..." Sharon looked down at the floor. "It came through about five minutes ago. I don't know. Everything has been a blur today."

"You think?" Emily snapped and Sharon flinched. "We

can't think. We need an exact time."

Emily leant over Sharon's shoulder then looked at her watch, calculating. Four minutes had already passed.

Chapter 54

Opening the timer application on her cell phone, Emily punched in seven minutes and twenty seconds. She checked the computer showed the same time as her watch. It was correct.

She hit the start button, and the timer began its countdown.

"How come you didn't mention he is your uncle?" Harry started. "That bastard has caused all this. If it wasn't for your family-"

"He," Emily pointed at the computer screen, "isn't my family. We're not even blood. He's nothing but a sworn enemy. If you want to clear your name, we need to get out of here. NOW."

Harry didn't flinch. All Emily saw was anger in his eyes and his knuckles turning white as he held his gun, tapping the side of his leg.

"Sharon, you're coming with me." Emily grabbed Sharon's arms and helped her out of her chair, placing herself in between her and Harry. "I'm not ready to die today and I hope you aren't, either. You have this one last chance to get out of here alive... If you stay, they may never recover your body. How do you think your family will feel about that? Your casket will be buried without a body in it.

"Your last chance." She felt behind her and pushed Sharon towards the door. "Sharon, get out of here. I'll be right behind you."

Harry raised his gun at Emily. Sharon ducked her head and ran out of the room.

"There'll be police down there, all guns pointing at us. They'll shoot me on sight."

"You don't want to do this. Do you want to see your family again? Do you want to walk your daughter down the aisle?"

A tear rolled down his cheek.

"Come on." Emily gestured for him to come. "Let's get out of here."

He lowered the gun and let it slowly drop through his fingers to the floor.

"Okay. You're good. Let's get out of here." Emily grabbed the nook in his elbow and pulled him out of the room.

"I'll try the elevator," Sharon yelled over her shoulder. Sharon was already at the end of the corridor. She pressed the button once, then punched it four more times, in rapid succession.

"That isn't going to help you. It won't be working today, not with the building leaning to one side. We'll need to take the stairs," Emily yelled.

"Stairs?" Sharon looked towards the emergency door then back at the elevator door.

Emily checked her watch. "Six minutes, thirty seconds left. Stairs. Now."

"Six floors, six minutes?" Sharon questioned.

Emily pushed them both towards the emergency exit.

"Whatever you do, don't stop. Keep running. Your life depends on it. Mind over matter."

Kicking the door in, she shoved them into the emergency stairwell.

Depressing the button on her handheld radio, Emily yelled into the microphone, "Schultz, we've got six minutes to get the hell out of this building."

The signal went static then Schultz's voice came over the radio frequency. "Can you repeat that?"

"Another video's been sent. We need to get the hell out of here, now."

"Fuck."

Then the radio was silent. Emily took one last look down the corridor before closing the door behind her.

"Hurry," Emily yelled out.

She grabbed the steel railing and a cold shiver traveled up her arm. Ignoring the sensation, she descended the steps two at a time. A door came into view, with a number five painted on it. Her heart pounded faster and louder. Her arms outstretched, she grabbed the curve in the railing with both hands and swung her body around. Missing the last few steps, she landed with a thump one the next set of steps.

Her phone beeped.

"Five minutes," she yelled to Harry and Sharon, who were just starting to descend level four stairs.

She didn't need to look at her phone. The timer was the only application active. The only app that mattered.

Emily noticed Sharon was starting to struggle, falling farther behind Harry.

"Schultz?" Emily said into her handheld radio. Static interference was her only reply. "Schultz. You there?"

No reply.

"Shit."

Sharon was bent over the railing, her breathing labored.

"Sharon. Listen to me." Emily pulled Sharon off the railing and held Sharon's head in her hands. "I really need you to push through the pain. Remember, mind over matter. Brain over muscle. Your body can do so much more than you think it can."

Sharon shook her head. "I... I... can't."

Emily grabbed Sharon by the arm and pulled her down the steps.

"Breathe. You need to calm your breathing down."

Sharon shook her head and let out a pitiful wail.

Emily gripped Sharon's arm tighter and picked up her pace.

Although Sharon's breathing was still labored, at least they were moving.

"Breathe through it." Emily practiced her deep breathing out loud, and Sharon mimicked her. Before they reached the next level, Sharon's breathing was under control.

"Much better. Now we need to pick up the pace a little."

"O-okay."

"We're getting out of here together. Right?"

"You don't have to wait for me. I know I'm holding you up. I've screwed up my life anyway. I've ruined what career I had. No one's going to want a secretary with my record. You've got your own family to worry about instead of me."

A vision of her sister and niece flashed before Emily. She fought back the tears.

"Don't talk bullshit. I'll personally put in a good word for you."

"Thank you." Sharon managed a small smile.

"Right. I don't leave anyone behind. Let's take these steps two at a time."

Without hesitating, Sharon took the lead, taking the steps two and sometimes three at a time. Emily followed close behind.

They reached the door to level two as her timer beeped again.

"Don't look back. Just keep running," Emily yelled out to Sharon.

Sharon stopped and looked back. Emily was holding the level two exit door open.

"Get going. I'll be right behind you. GO. NOW."

She looked at her phone. Two minutes.

Holding the door open, she yelled out, "Schultz." This was the last level she'd heard Schultz mention on the radio. He must be here somewhere, unless he was already outside and clear of the building.

Level two appeared very much like level six. A long corridor with doors on either side and a common area at the end. A few shadows moving at the other end caught her attention.

She tried her radio again. "Schultz."

There was static then his familiar voice appeared. "Lee?"

"Where are you?"

"Level two."

"What are you still doing up here? You've now got two minutes. Get out of there. NOW."

"We're coming."

"You're wasting time. I've got Harry and Sharon. They're already on their way down."

Schultz appeared at the end of the corridor.

"We're just clearing the last of this floor," he relayed over the radio.

"I see you're leaving it to the last minute again."

He stayed where he was and waved everyone through while Emily held the door open and gestured for them to hurry towards her.

"Quick, quick," she told them as they run past.

"You need to come, too." One of them grabbed her arm.

She held her ground and pulled her arm back. "I'll be right behind you. I promise."

He let go and joined his team. Schultz followed soon behind and pushed her through the door.

They took the steps a few at a time. In between leaps, Schultz asked, "Your uncle up to his old tricks again?"

"Funny way of putting it."

Emily's phone beeped.

As she ran down the stairs, she pulled it out of her back pocket. Schultz tried to look over his shoulder at her phone, where bright red double-digit numbers flashed.

"How long?"

"We're down to seconds." She slipped her phone back into her pocket. "Unless you want this building to be your tomb, I'd get moving. NOW."

Chapter 55

The ground level door was within reach. Emily was now a few steps in front of Schultz. She grabbed the door as the last of the men ran through it.

Her phone beeped, and Emily ignored it. A second later it beeped again. This time she pulled it out.

The numbers on the screen flashed 0:14.

"Schultz, ten seconds."

"Seriously?"

Just the width of the building to go. The first of the uniforms were clearing the front doors. Clenching her jaws tight, Emily pushed her legs to a new level of pain and sprinted across the ground level floor. She felt like she was running a one-mile dash, and the shiny tiled floor wasn't helping her get there any quicker.

Reaching the rotating doors, she pushed the one closest to her. The door remained shut.

"Come on," she pushed it again.

"This way." Schultz pushed the door in the opposite direction and the door began to roll around.

She was monitoring the automatic moving doors, waiting for the perfect time to step in between the glass doors, when she was shoved in. Hobbling on her right foot, she quickly rebalanced herself and looked back to where she had been standing only a moment before. Schultz winked at her before he stepped in the door space behind hers.

The beeps on her phone were one solid tone now.

Stepping outside onto the steps of the building, Emily felt the ground rumble. Without looking back to ensure Schultz was following, she sprinted across the tiled platform.

Boom.

Emily felt her body lift and fly through the air. The ground hurtled towards her. Unable to hear anything, she closed her eyes and braced her arms over her face and head. Debris belted into her back.

She landed with a thud and lost count of the number of times she rolled down the road. Debris rained around her as she lay there too stunned to move, the ringing in her ears throbbing through her head.

Out of the corner of her eye, she caught a shadow pass over her. Had Fu's men caught up with her, finally, just as she'd gotten away? Closing her eyes, she held her breath, waiting for the pain to end.

She counted down from ten to zero, expecting to feel the barrel of a gun on her temple. She slowly lifted one eyelid. There was no one in front of her.

Closing her eye again, she lay still, her breathing slowed right down. She counted three heartbeats before she took another breath.

She jumped when she felt a blanket being placed over her. A hand appeared and tucked the blanket around her front and under her chin. The warmth gave her a sense of security and comfort despite her world being silent.

A paramedic knelt in front of her. His lips moved. Emily frowned, trying helplessly to lip-read but failing. She shrugged her shoulders and grimaced from the excruciating pain shooting down her arm. She tried to move her other arm over and hold her sore shoulder but it was pinned under her body.

The paramedic held a green plastic stick in front of him and pretended to suck on it. He gestured it towards her. Emily looked between him and the plastic stick. He nodded at her and moved it in front of her. With her pinned hand she grabbed it and moved her fingers along to the end of the stick until it reached her mouth. The paramedic demonstrated a deep inhale and Emily followed suit.

She exhaled and inhaled again, and felt the pain slowly dulling.

Schultz, her thoughts screamed.

Emily looked up at the paramedic, pressing her thumb and index finger together, like she was holding a pencil. She pretended to scribble.

The paramedic pulled a notepad and pencil out of his shirt pocket and handed it to Emily. With her good arm, she scrawled "Schultz?" onto the notepad and turned it around to show the paramedic.

The paramedic gestured for her to hand the pencil back to him. Emily handed it over and he turned to the next page and scribbled something down before handing it back to her.

She read it. His writing was much neater than hers. "We're still attending to everyone. I'll let you know as soon as I know."

Her heart ached. She'd never felt so alone before.

She scribbled "Please" underneath his message and showed him.

After reading it, he nodded, and a small smile appeared on his face. Although nice and somewhat comforting, it still wasn't the same. It wasn't Schultz's smile warming her, ensuring she was safe and comfortable.

Calm and sleep began to sweep over her. She smiled thinking about whatever was in that green stick; it was doing something wonderful for her.

She was startled out of her doze when she felt her body being moved. Her eyes shot open. She was being placed on a white linen bed.

She scrambled around for the notebook and found it tucked under her arm, together with the pencil. Flipping through to the first page, she held it up to the paramedic standing alongside her.

His grin spread from one ear to the other.

Emily flicked through the notepad to the next empty page and scribbled down, "Safe?"

The paramedic nodded, and she relaxed.

Emily felt every bump as they wheeled her away. She turned towards the building but another paramedic was blocking her view. He held the side of the bed with one hand, and in the other hand he had an intravenous bag with a tube. Following the clear tube, she saw it running into her hand.

She raised her head a little, resting on her good arm. Ahead of her at least four ambulances lined up along the intersection.

Emily was wheeled past the first ambulance, where she glimpsed Sharon being checked over by a paramedic. From the way she was moving, Emily could tell she appeared to have fared well. Only a few scratches were visible on her upper body. Sharon caught her eye, returned her thumbs-up, and mouthed "Thank you," with her fist tapping her chest.

As they wheeled her past the second ambulance, Emily held up her opened hand. The paramedics kept pushing her gurney. She frantically wrote down, "STOP. PLEASE," and held it up for them to see.

They stopped.

She scribbled in the book, "It'll be okay," and held it up. Harry went to take a step towards her but was held back. He pulled his arm again. It wasn't moving. Emily looked down and saw he was handcuffed to the ambulance.

"Don't fight it. We'll be in touch. OK?" she wrote and held it up for him to read.

"I'm sorry," he mouthed to her before sitting on the back of the ambulance.

She was on the move again.

The paramedics stopped outside the third ambulance without her needing to ask them. Emily scanned its interior but didn't see anyone sitting on its end or lying down in it. Perhaps this one was hers. She waited for the paramedics to turn her gurney and wheel her in. But she didn't move. Instead, the paramedics walked to the rear of the ambulance and a moment later they were helping someone out.

They were staggering, trying to keep their balance as the occupant struggled to step out. Standing on firm ground, he looked up at her.

Fighting through the pain, Emily sat upright and extended her uninjured arm. Schultz tried to run but grimaced and blanched when he stood on his left leg. The paramedics braced him as he hobbled over to her.

Two steps away from her, he spoke to the paramedic and he stepped aside. Schultz took the last two shaky steps by himself, then fell into her open arms and held her tight. Emily felt her pain dissolve as he held her.

Eventually, Schultz pulled away. His eyes were watering up. She smiled and used the side of her good thumb to wipe his tears away. He held her hand tight before placing a kiss on it.

Remembering her notebook, Emily pulled her hand away, pointed one finger in the air and mouthed, "One minute."

She turned the page and scribbled, "You're alive!"

Schultz read it, and she saw him lean back and laugh.

She realized at that point how silly that would've looked. Of course he was alive. She drew a heavy line through it and thought for a couple of seconds, trying to find the perfect words.

But Schultz grabbed the book and wrote something down. He closed the book and handed it back to her. Before Emily had a chance to do anything, he patted the paramedic near him on the back and she was on the move again.

Emily tilted her head, keeping Schultz in her sight for as long as possible. He stood there, hobbling on his leg. Their eyes locked.

Her bed was rolled around and she was loaded into the next ambulance. A tear rolled down her face as Schultz disappeared from view.

A few jerky movements later as the paramedics lined the bed up with the rollers inside the ambulance, she was secured inside. The paramedic who'd been with her all along sat on the bed opposite her and placed a cuff over her bicep. The doors closed and she felt the faint sway as the van began to move.

Pulling the notebook out, she flicked through the pages until she came across the message Schultz had just written.

It read, "You'll be in my arms again soon."

Closing the notebook and holding it tight, Emily felt a smile creep across her face. She closed her eyes and drifted to sleep.

Chapter 56

Two days later Emily knocked on Schultz's office door, her hospital bracelet still dangling from her left wrist.

She was feeling a lot better now, after a couple of days' rest and back in her own clothes. Schultz's office had been her first stop after being given her discharge papers and proper wound care.

"Come in," his muffled voice sounded through the closed door.

Emily peered in and saw he was on the phone. She mouthed "Sorry" and backed out of the room.

Schultz clicked his fingers and Emily peered back around the edge of the door. He gestured to her it was okay and to sit down on one of the vacant chairs opposite him.

Hobbling over, she noticed how fresh he looked, like he hadn't been caught up in the attack. She pulled the chair back, making it scrape along the tiled floor.

"So sorry," she whispered.

"Thank you, Commissioner. Yes, I'll pass on the information." Schultz hung up the phone.

Emily hobbled on her good foot as she lowered herself onto the seat.

Schultz leant back in his chair and closed his eyes. A look of worry crept over his face, which he tried to hide by rubbing his hands over his face. It didn't work.

"What's happened?" Emily asked.

Leaning forward, Schultz looked at her, his face grim.

"Schultz, talk to me."

The corner of his eyes crinkled upwards as a smile emerged.

"Been a crazy few days, hasn't it?" Schultz walked to the corner kitchenette and poured hot water into pre-prepared coffee cups.

"Yeah. You could say that." She smiled as he passed a coffee to her. "Not the phone call you were expecting?" She nodded towards the phone.

"Maybe."

"Come on. What aren't you tellin' me?"

"You going to lay low for a while?" Schultz sat down, passing her a package over the desk.

Emily grabbed it and chuckled. "You know me. What's this?"

"Recovered from the boat yard. Our guys have no reason

to keep it. It's yours, isn't it?"

Emily hugged her handbag to her chest and nodded, grateful.

Schultz took a sip from his coffee cup before continuing. "That was the big boss on the phone. You've certainly stirred up the pot this time."

"Just doing my job."

"Only this time it wasn't your job, was it? Your boss didn't assign that case to anyone."

"Yeah, well, a little extra-curricular project hasn't killed anyone. Well, not yet, anyway."

Schultz coughed and spluttered on the mouthful of coffee he'd just sipped.

Grabbing a bunch of tissues from beside his monitor, he began to mop up the coffee spray. "I've just been informed there's going to be a full investigation into the banking sector, which may lead to a total sector overhaul. Foreign investments in Australia are also going to be reviewed."

"That's a start. But it isn't going to help the farmers right now. They're the ones who are living through this."

"No. No, it's not." He threw the coffee-soaked tissues in the trashcan under his desk. "A joint independent and government committee is being established as we speak."

"Another one? One that'll probably be tainted by people from the banking sector." Emily snorted out a fake laugh, shaking her head. "What's this whiz-bang committee going to solve?"

"At least something is being done." His tone was dead

serious. "While they're conducting their investigations, they'll also be overseeing all land and property transfers for Victoria. No transfer can be completed without their seal of approval."

"Right," Emily replied, sounding unconvinced.

"Anything is better than nothing."

"Suppose. What about Harry?"

Schultz sipped his coffee.

"His farm will be returned to his family in the coming weeks. When they're ready, we're allowing them back on their property."

"That's good to hear. But that's not all, is it?"

"No, it's not." Schultz was unable to look at her.

"Don't tell me they're going to press charges against him."

"There'll be a full investigation into everything. I suspect the events leading up to the siege will be taken into consideration."

"Is he a suspect?"

"We won't know until the end."

Emily looked at him, confused.

"I'm not on the case," Schultz continued. "With my involvement this week, I'm too close."

"That sucks. You're one of their leading detectives."

"It is what it is. It's going to be a big case. I don't think anyone realizes just how big, yet."

Emily raised an eyebrow.

"You know the evidence you gave us?" Emily nodded and Schultz continued. "It's massive."

"Exactly how big are we talking?"

"Put it this way. Unless they employ more technical personnel to assist in these cases, I'll probably be retired by the time any of it gets anywhere close to getting in front of a judge."

Emily's eyes widened.

"Are you saying Harry may never receive a hearing?"

Schultz shrugged a shoulder and raised an eyebrow.

"What about all the other farmers who've been affected?"

"They'll take a little longer, as the transfers were already completed. But at this stage it appears they'll get their properties back, as well. The research you've done, and Harry standing up for something he believed in, have caused your unc- I mean the syndicate has taken a huge hit in their investment portfolio."

Emily blushed.

"There's always a job here for you." Schultz winked at her. "Words from the Commissioner."

Laughing, Emily replied, "You know I'm no good at following orders and staying in line. I'm a free spirit."

"Can't blame a guy for trying. So, what are you going to do? Protective custody is still on the table. With Fu out there and now one of our most wanted, you are still in danger."

"He may be my uncle on paper, but to me he's a nobody. I'll take my chances out there. Anyway, what are the chances he'll find me? It's a big world."

"Brian's still on the loose, too."

"I'll be all right. They won't expect me to pop up in Russia." She smiled. "After the funeral, I'll be jet-packing back overseas. I believe I have a couple of weeks to organize my matters before my new assignment begins. I might even get my white Christmas while I'm there."

"You'd better pack your coats and boots."

"Already packed. Actually, I haven't even unpacked my suitcases yet."

Emily watched on as Schultz shifted in his seat, his eyes on his coffee.

"What aren't you telling me?"

"No." He waved his hand. "It's nothing."

"Come on. Spit it out."

His phone vibrated on his desk. Out of the corner of his eye he looked at the screen and returned to his coffee cup.

"The Commissioner has strongly advised that I'm to use up some of my annual leave and long service allowance. They reckon it's exactly twelve months."

"Okay. So why don't you? It's been a while since you've had a break."

His police-issued phone vibrated again.

"You gonna get that?" Emily nodded at the phone. "It's okay, you are still on the clock."

Schultz sighed as he picked up his phone. Unlocking it, he paused.

"Looks like I'm not going be going on leave after all."

Emily looked at him confused. "Huh?"

Schultz handed the phone over. Emily kept her face as straight as she could. The number, she recognized all too well.

"I'm wanted in Russia, too?"

Author Notes

I can't thank you enough for not only picking up this book but for reading it all the way to the end. Thank you!

Although I come from a career in accounting and business management, I've always been a creative at heart and when it came to writing my first series it made sense for me to blend the two together and Emily Lee was born.

The Analyst took me a little longer than I'd anticipated to complete as I scraped the initial seven thousand or so words and started again, putting more action up front. But, I've loved the journey as I've re-connected with my writing.

I'm not usually a detailed planner and this book was no exception. I had maybe a few early scenes but that was it and I tried to flesh out the story before I started writing it but

Emily had other ideas, so I was surprised when Schultz, and Fu popped up like they did. They've concreted where the series is going, unless they change their minds along the way and steer this series in a different direction.

If you enjoyed The Analyst, you'll be happy to know book two, which has a working title of The Manager, is going through its final read through before being sent to the editor and I've already started writing book three which has a working title of The Inheritance.

What I can tell you is Schultz will be accompanying Emily in Book Two and Fu, well he'll be in the background, watching and waiting for the right moment to resurface.

Beyond these first three books, future instalments are planned for Emily Lee. With plans already underway for a separate series that may (or may not) be connected to The Emily Lee Series— we'll have to wait and see!

If you enjoyed this book, please give it a good rating on Amazon, Goodreads or where you usually leave reviews. It's these ratings that help future readers when they're looking for a new book or author to dive into.

Thank you for reading The Analyst, the first book in my debut series!

Follow me

If you'd like to be kept up to date on new releases please subscribe to my email list at:

www.kabragonje.com

You can also connect with me on the following platforms:

Amazon www.amazon.com/author/kabragonje

Facebook www.facebook.com/kabragonje

Instagram www.instagram.com/kabragonje

Acknowledgments

My writers' journey from planning to completion may appear to be solitary but behind the scene there's a great team of individuals who've helped make my dream a reality.

I'd like to say thank you first and foremost for the support provided by my family from husband and children, my parents, brother and sisters. They're my personal cheer squad and their support kept me moving forward, allowed me to believe in myself when I was having doubts. Thank you all for believing in me.

I'm not a crazy cat lady, I swear, but thank you to our cat Rita for keeping me company into the early hours of the night while I punched out the words.

I'd like to say thank you to my editor Ella, your initial response when you returned my first draft spurred me on. You've also seen this book go through a few drafts and this book is now a lot better because of your skill and time. Even if you were tearing your hair out because Xander was simply referred to as 'X' in the first draft.

Thank you, Olivia for the cover art, you've made the whole process stress free. I gave you a bare bone description of the book and you turned that into a great cover!

I cannot forget the very supportive indie author support groups I belong to. I've been following all your journey's as you've travelled the indie author trail before me, learning and letting us all know what does and doesn't work. Your inspiration and support have allowed me to chase and live my life long dream. Thank you, ladies and gents!

To anyone who knows a writer, do not underestimate the power of your encouragement.

www.ingramcontent.com/pod-product-compliance
Lightning Source LLC
Chambersburg PA
CBHW021405110726
47901CB00008B/2068